Louise Fuller was once a tomboy who hated pink and always wanted to be the Prince—not the Princess! Now she enjoys creating heroines who aren't pretty push-overs but strong, believable women. Before writing for Mills & Boon she studied literature and philosophy at university, and then worked as a reporter on her local newspaper. She lives in Tunbridge Wells with her impossibly handsome husband Patrick and their six children.

Also by Louise Fuller

Vows Made in Secret
A Deal Sealed by Passion
Claiming His Wedding Night
Blackmailed Down the Aisle
Kidnapped for the Tycoon's Baby
Surrender to the Ruthless Billionaire
Revenge at the Altar
Demanding His Secret Son

Discover more at millsandboon.co.uk.

CONSEQUENCES OF A HOT HAVANA NIGHT

LOUISE FULLER

MILLS & BOON

First Published in Great Britain 2019
by Mills & Boon, an imprint of HarperCollins*Publishers*
1 London Bridge Street, London, SE1 9GF

© 2019 Louise Fuller

ISBN: 978-0-263-27090-7

MIX
Paper from
responsible sources
FSC® C007454

This book is produced from independently certified FSC™ paper
to ensure responsible forest management.
For more information visit www.harpercollins.co.uk/green.

Printed and bound in Spain
by CPI, Barcelona

To Aggie:
For allowing me to relive the eighties and nineties
(go Buffy!),
and for trying hard at the things you find hardest.
All my love. X

CHAPTER ONE

GAZING OUT AT the sun-soaked, shimmering turquoise sea, Kitty Quested held her breath.

It was strange to imagine that this water might one day be curling onto the shingle beach near her home in England. But then, even now, nearly four weeks after arriving in Cuba, everything still felt a little strange. Not just the sea, or the beach—this incredible scimitar of silvery sand—but the fact that for now this was her home.

Home.

Lifting the mass of long, copper-coloured curls to cool her neck, she felt her throat start to ache as she imagined the small coastal village in the south of England where up until a month ago she'd lived out her whole life.

Birth.

Marriage.

And the death of her childhood sweetheart and husband Jimmy.

Pushing back the brim of her hat to see better, she blinked into the sunlight as a light breeze lifted her hair, blowing fresh against her cheek and reminding her of everything she'd left behind.

Her parents, her sister Lizzie and her boyfriend Bill, a two-month tenancy on a one-bedroom terraced cottage overlooking the sea. And her job at Bill's start-up, distilling what had become their first product: Blackstrap Rum.

She felt a sharp pang of homesickness.

When Miguel Mendoza, director of operations at Dos Rios Rum, had called her three months ago to discuss the possibility of her creating two new flavours for the brand's two hundredth anniversary, she'd never imagined that it would lead to her moving four thousand miles across the Atlantic Ocean.

If she'd allowed himself to think about it she would have refused. She'd been flattered to be asked but, unlike Lizzie, she was by nature cautious, and the hand she'd been dealt in life had taught her to be wary. Accepting the Dos Rios job would not just boost her salary, it would mean leaving everything and everyone she'd ever known. But, five years after Jimmy's illness and death had put her life on hold, change was what she wanted and thought she needed in order to put her grief behind her and start living again.

So, five minutes after putting the phone down, she'd called him back and said yes.

And she didn't regret her decision. Her new home, a white single-storey villa, was beautiful, and only a short walk from the beach. Everyone was friendly, and after three years in Bill's cramped stillroom, working in the vast state-of-the-art Dos Rios lab felt like a treat. In so many ways it was absolutely the fresh start she'd imagined. She'd made new friends and was building a career. But one part of her life remained untouched—

Her throat tightened.

And it was going to stay untouched.

Reaching up, she captured the dark red hair spilling over her shoulders and down her back. At the airport she'd promised her sister that she would 'let her hair down'. It was an old joke between them, because normally she tied it up, here in Cuba though she had started to let it hang free.

But her hair was one thing...her heart was another entirely.

Jimmy had been her first love, and she couldn't imagine feeling about any man the way she had felt about him. Nor did she want to. Love, *real* love, was both a lightness and a weight, a gift and a burden, one that she didn't have it in her to give or receive any more. Of course, nobody really believed her—her friends and family were convinced that it was just grief talking—but she knew that part of her life was over, and no amount of sunshine or salsa was going to change that fact.

Glancing down into the water, she felt her pulse jump as she spotted a cantaloupe-coloured starfish floating serenely in the gin-clear shallows.

Starfish! What was that in Spanish? she wondered. It wasn't the kind of word she'd learned in the lessons she'd been taking back home—the lessons that had seemed less like a hobby and more like fate when Dos Rios had offered her this four-month contract.

Star was *estrella* and fish was *pescado*, but that didn't sound quite right. If only Lizzie was here to help. Her sister had studied Spanish and French at university and had a natural affinity for languages, whereas her own dyslexia had made even learning English a challenge.

Pulling out her phone, she was just about to look up the word when it began to vibrate.

Her lips curved upwards. Speak of the devil! It was Lizzie.

'Are your ears burning?' she asked.

'No! But my feet are soaking wet. Will that do?'

Hearing her sister's burst of laughter, Kitty started to smile. 'Why are your feet wet?'

'It's not just my feet. I'm soaked through. And please don't tell me that you miss the rain!'

'I wasn't going to,' Kitty protested—although she did, actually.

'You were thinking it.'

Kitty laughed. 'It must be quite a downpour if you got that wet going from the house to the car.'

'The car wouldn't start so I had to walk to the station. I missed my train, and then the next train was held up, and the waiting room was closed for renovations, so me and all the other poor sad wage-slaves just had to stand on the platform and get wet.'

'I thought you were going to get a new car?'

'And when we need to, we will.' Lizzie spoke calmly. 'So stop fretting and tell me why my ears should be on fire?'

Kitty felt the tightness in her chest ease. Lizzie and Bill had basically supported her, not just emotionally but financially, for the last four years. When Jimmy had been admitted into the hospice she had moved into Lizzie's spare room, and after his death Bill had asked her to help him with his latest venture—a micro rum distillery.

It had been an act of kindness and love. They hadn't really been able to afford her salary, and she'd had no experience and nothing to offer except a degree in chemistry.

She could never truly repay them, but after all the sacrifices Lizzie had made the least she could do was convince her sister that they had been worthwhile and that her new life was fabulous.

'I wanted to know what the Spanish word is for starfish,' she said quickly. 'And I thought you'd know.'

'I do—it's *estrella de mar*. But why do you need to know?' Lizzie hesitated. 'Please tell me you're not adding starfish to the rum? Bill and I ate them in China—on sticks like lollipops—and I really don't recommend it.'

Kitty screwed up her face. 'That is gross—and, no, of course I'm not going to put starfish in the rum. I just keep seeing them in the sea.'

She heard her sister groan. 'You're looking at one right now, aren't you? Shouldn't you be at work? Or have I got my times wrong again?'

Kitty grinned. 'I'm not in the office, but this *is* work. I'm doing research.'

Lizzie said a very rude word that her mother had once sent Kitty to her room for saying.

'Well, I just hope you're covering up. You know how easily you burn.'

Glancing down at her long-sleeved blouse and maxi-skirt, Kitty sighed. 'The sun isn't that hot now, but I'm wearing so much clothing and sunblock I'm probably going to come back paler than when I left anyway.'

'Who knows? You might not come back at all. Not if that gorgeous boss of yours finally decides to pay a visit to his hometown and your eyes meet across a deserted boardroom...'

Hearing the teasing note in her sister's voice, Kitty shook her head. For all her pragmatism, Lizzie was actually a committed believer in love at first sight—but then she had every reason to be, having met Bill in a karaoke bar in Kyoto on her gap year.

Kitty, on the other hand, had not even had to leave her house to meet Jimmy. He'd lived next door and they'd met before they'd even been able to walk, when his mother had invited her mother over for tea one afternoon when they were just babies.

'I work in the labs, Lizzie. I don't even know where the boardroom is. And even if he does come to Havana, I don't suppose my "gorgeous boss" will even know who I am, much less care.'

After she'd hung up, having promised to call later, Kitty made her way back up the beach to the forest that edged the sand. It was always cooler there than anywhere else.

She wasn't rushing—and not just because the pine needles were slippery to walk on. It was just how people did things in Cuba. Even at work everyone moved at a pace of their own making, and after a week of replicating her typical English nine-to-five day she'd surrendered to 'Cuban' time. It had felt odd at first, but the sky hadn't come crashing down—and, as Mr Mendoza had told her the first time they'd spoken—she was her own boss.

But as she made her way along a path edged with sea grape and tamarind trees, her cheeks felt suddenly warm. What was she talking about?

Like everything else on this untouched peninsula, these trees, the beach, probably even the starfish, were all part of the Finca el Pinar Zayas estate. A private estate that belonged to *el jefazo*—the big boss, as his staff referred to him.

César Zayas y Diago.

His name was not so much a name as a spell. Rolling her tongue over the exotic syllables, she felt her stomach tighten nervously, as though even thinking them inside her head might have the power to conjure the man himself to this deserted woodland.

Some hope!

Lizzie might imagine that she was going to cross paths with the Dos Rios boss, but so far she hadn't even spoken to him on the phone. He'd copied her in on some emails, and she'd received a letter of congratulations allegedly from him when her contract had been finalised, but realistically it was unlikely that he'd even seen it.

Somehow she couldn't imagine the elusive, work-hungry, publicity-shy CEO sitting in the penthouse office of his company headquarters, chewing his pen and trying to find exactly the right words to toast her success. And that signature that she'd spent so long examining had probably been perfected by one of his personal assistants a long time ago.

Not that she was bothered at his lack of interest. In fact, she was quite relieved.

She had moved from the quiet English coast to the pulsing heart of the Caribbean, but she was still a small-town girl, and meeting her legendary and no doubt formidable boss was an experience she was happy to miss.

And he must feel the same way about meeting her, because he had visited the head office twice since she'd arrived, and both times he had left before she had even realised he was in the country.

Truthfully, though, she hadn't been expecting to

meet him. He might have a beautiful Colonial-style home on the estate, and the site of the original distillery was the Dos Rios headquarters, but his business took him all over the world. According to her colleagues, he visited Havana infrequently, and rarely stayed more than a couple of days.

Of course she was curious about him—who wouldn't be? He had taken a modest, family-owned rum distillery and turned it into a global brand. And, unlike so many of his business peers, he had done so at the same time as refusing to play the media game.

She ducked under an overhanging branch, wondering why it was that despite his phenomenal success César Zayas's private life was so private. If he was famous for anything aside from his rum, it was for the way he guarded his privacy with almost pit-bull determination.

Perhaps he was just modest. His biography on the Dos Rios website certainly implied that: it was brief to the point of being minimalist. There were no personal comments or inspirational quotes, just a couple of lines hidden in a more general piece about the history of the company.

Even the photo accompanying the piece seemed designed not to inform but to mislead anyone looking to find out more about the man behind the brand. He was standing in the centre of a group of men lounging on a veranda, glasses of *ron* in their hands, the colour of the liquid an exact match for the huge burnt orange sun setting behind them. It was an informal shot, but it perfectly captured their camaraderie and their glorious masculine swagger.

They were casually dressed, shirtsleeves rolled up, collars loosened, arms resting on each other's shoulders. Some were laughing, some holding the island's other famous export—the Cuban cigar.

All were gazing at the camera.

All except one.

Remembering the picture, Kitty felt her mouth grow dry.

The Dos Rios CEO was turning away, so that his face was slightly blurred, and it was possible only to sense the flawless cheekbones and sculpted jawline beneath the smudge of dark stubble and tousled black hair.

There was no key to identify who was who, but it didn't matter. Even blurred, his features and the clean lines of his buttoned-up and clearly expensive shirt were stamped with an unmistakable air of privilege, that sense of having the world at his feet. For him, life would always be bright and easy and fast—too fast for the shutter speed of any camera.

Only his smile—a smile she had never seen but could easily imagine—would be slow...slow and languorous like a long, cool daiquiri.

She swallowed, almost tasting the hit of rum and the tang of lime on her tongue.

Except she didn't drink daiquiris. Daiquiris were cocktails, and she had never felt cool or confident enough to order one. Not even here in Cuba.

Especially not here in Cuba.

Everyone was so beautiful and sun-kissed and happy. The men had dark, narrowed gazes and moved like panthers, and the women made even the simplest actions—crossing the road, buying fruit at the market—look as though they were dancing the Mambo.

She hadn't dared to face Havana at night, but she had visited three times during daylight and she could still

feel the vibrancy of the city humming in her chest—
drowsy but dangerous, like a swarm of bees. She'd been
captivated not just by the people but by the faded rev-
olutionary slogans on the walls promising *Revolución
para Siempre*—Revolution For Ever—and the Pantone
palette of gleaming, buffed *máquinas*, the classic nine-
teen-fifties American cars that lined every street.

Everywhere there were reminders of the past from
elaborate, Colonial-style balconies to curving marble
staircases. It was vivid, and exhilarating, and she had
been tempted to press herself against the hot stucco and
absorb some of the lambent warmth of the city into her
blood before heading off to explore the tangle of alleys
leading off the main squares.

Only she had a terrible sense of direction.

Speaking of which—

She had reached a fork in the path, and she stopped
and glanced hesitantly in both directions.

There was no point trying to use her phone—the
signal was only strong enough right by the sea—and
it was impossible to see over the tops of the pine trees
that gave the estate its name. If she went the wrong way
it would take for ever. She'd just have to make her way
to the track-cum-road that led through the estate and
then she'd know where she was.

She felt her heart begin to beat faster.

Her villa was at the edge of the estate. Usually it
was home to one of the maids who worked at the main
house, but she had gone to the other side of the island to
take care of her sick mother, so it was currently empty.
She'd been told by Andreas, the head of Dos Rios security, that she was welcome to explore the estate, but
she had mostly stuck to the beach and woods around

the house. She had never gone as the far as the road before, not on foot anyway.

It took less than ten minutes, and as she stepped between the trees onto the edge of the track she knew immediately where she was. Thank goodness. From here, her villa was only ten minutes away.

Breathing out in relief, she lifted up her hat and fanned her face—and then froze. Half hidden by the dark green vegetation, sunlight dappling their backs, were a group of the wild horses that roamed the estate.

Her heart gave a thump. She knew from conversations with Melenne, who came in three times a week to clean the *cabaña*, that the horses were not wild in the sense of dangerous, they were just not 'broken'. They moved freely, foraging in the woods, and it showed in their satin-smooth coats and toned muscles.

They were so beautiful, she thought, feeling a lump building in her throat, and tentatively, slowly, she took a step closer, holding out her hand to the nearest one. She held her breath as he gazed at her assessingly, and then her pulse darted as his soft, velvety nose snuffled against her fingers.

Breathing out cautiously, she held her hand steady—and then suddenly there was a rumbling growl from behind her, and as one the horses turned and wheeled away between the trees.

What the—?

Turning round towards the noise, Kitty lifted her hand to shield her face as a burst of sunlight hit her eyes. The noise swelled into a roar and there was a gleam of metal. She gasped, the sound choking off as a motorbike and its rider reared up in front of her. She got just the briefest impression of dark eyes narrowing in surprise, and then everything seemed to go into slow motion as the bike swerved away from her, skidding, tilting sideways, sliding smoothly across the coarse-packed dirt until finally it came to a shuddering stop.

For a moment, time contracted to a heartbeat.

Was he hurt?

Was he—?

She couldn't even think the word—and she pushed it away. She was struggling to breathe, her brain scrabbling, her mind stunned, disbelieving what had just happened. And then something opened inside of her chest, and even as panic jostled with fear she was running towards the bike.

The rider was already on his knees, and as he clambered to his feet he glanced up at her and swore in Spanish under his breath—or at least she assumed by the tone of his voice that he was swearing. Her Spanish lessons had been more focused on conjugating verbs than on cursing.

As she reached the bike she stopped and glanced back down the road, stomach clenching. From here it was possible to see clearly in both directions. Had she been standing on this spot she would have seen the bike, and he would have seen her, and the accident would never have happened.

The randomness of it made her head spin. In contrast, the motorcyclist seemed remarkably unperturbed.

Watching him, she felt her skin start to prickle. He was pressing his hand against the chassis of the bike as though it was one of the horses he'd startled, making the muscles beneath his oddly formal white shirt strain against the poplin.

He looked so vivid and real and she hated that he

might have been hurt; hated too that she had unwittingly played a part in his accident. If only she had been standing where she was now. But then she would never have met him—this man.

Her breathing jerked as the thought sneaked into her head from nowhere and refused to leave.

It had been a long time since a member of the opposite sex had even registered on her radar, but this man resonated.

Out of the corner of her eye she noticed the underside of the bike's wheel, still spinning slowly, and she was grateful for the reminder of what had so nearly happened and how she should react, for otherwise her brain might not have remembered what passed for acceptable behaviour.

'Are you okay?'

He lifted his gaze and for a moment she forgot to breathe as dark green eyes the same colour as the pine trees behind her stared at her in confusion. And then she realised she was speaking in English.

She blinked. 'Sorry, I mean...*se hecho daño*?'

He shook his head slowly, his gaze fixed on her face, and she saw that his expression had shifted from confusion to something like irritation. Instantly the sick panic she'd felt at watching the bike's wheels slide from under him was replaced by a bubbling rush of anger.

'*Cómo*—? I mean, *puede*—? Oh, what's the word?' She broke off in frustration. She was too angry to think straight in her own language, let alone in Spanish.

'That would depend, I suppose, on what it is you're trying to say.'

Her stomach clenched. He was speaking English—fluent, almost accentless English.

But clinging onto her outrage, she pushed past her astonishment. 'How could you be so reckless? You could have been hurt. Or worse,' she said accusingly.

'Unlikely. I wasn't going that fast. Besides...' He paused and then almost casually hoisted up the right leg of his trousers and showed her a thin, knotted scar running up from his ankle. 'I've done far worse.'

She gaped at him in silence, too stunned to respond and dazzled not just by the effortless way he switched between languages but by his casual lack of concern for his own safety. A sliver of anger she didn't really understand twisted inside her as she watched him lean over the bike and haul it upright, nudging out the kickstand with his foot.

'How about you?'

He still hadn't turned to face her, but as he glanced over a jolt like a pulse of electricity passed between them as his eyes locked onto hers, his green gaze so intent she felt flushed and dizzy.

'Are *you* okay?'

She stared at him blankly. He sounded business-like rather than concerned, but she barely registered his words. She was too distracted by his face. Caught in the sunlight, it was beautiful. The straight nose and jaw were outlined in gold, his skin clear and bright like a just lit flame.

Like a just lit flame?

She felt herself tremble as the words echoed inside her head. Thankfully she'd only thought them and not actually said them out loud, but what was she thinking?

Easy question.

Wrong answer.

She was thinking about his mouth and how it would feel pressed against hers.

She frowned, flustered by her unexpected and unwelcome reaction to a stranger—a stranger who had scant regard both for himself and the safety of others. A stranger who couldn't even be bothered to turn and face her.

Her heart began to beat faster, and she had a sudden impulse to turn and dart back beneath the trees. Only there was something in her that wanted to know what would happen if she stayed.

'I'm fine. Although I'm surprised you're bothering to ask.'

She spoke quickly, her words tumbling over themselves, for she was not by nature a confrontational person—a character trait that had only been reinforced by months of sitting in hospital waiting rooms and dealing with a conveyor belt of compassionate but phlegmatic specialists and consultants.

But something about this man...something in his manner...sparked against her like a match striking tinder.

He tipped his head back, his lips parting slightly as though internally questioning what he'd just heard.

'What is that supposed to mean?'

He spoke softly, but there was an edge to his voice that made the hairs stand up on her arms. But remembering how the wild horses had scattered at his approach, her irritation was rekindled and she felt the last of her panic disappear in the face of his level gaze.

'It means that you almost ran into me.'

His eyes flashed, the whites glinting like teeth, but his gaze stayed locked on her face. 'Yes, because you stepped out in front of me. I only came off the bike because I had to swerve to avoid hitting you.'

Her cheeks coloured and she hesitated. It was true, she *had* stepped out into the road... But, glancing back at him, she gritted her teeth. He wasn't even wearing a helmet. How could he be so arrogant, so blasé?

Suddenly her whole body was shaking. She had a sharp, vivid memory of Jimmy, sitting on the sofa in his pyjamas, his face grey with exhaustion, and her heart began to pound with anger. Jimmy had lived his life so carefully, and yet here was this man—this arrogant, reckless man—taking stupid risks, taunting fate, challenging his own mortality.

'Well, you wouldn't have had to swerve if you hadn't been going so fast,' she said hotly, gesturing towards his scarred leg. 'Which is clearly something you make a habit of doing.'

'Like I said, I wasn't going fast. This is a brand-new bike.' He gave her a disparaging glance. 'I only picked it up today, so I'm still breaking it in.' Eyes narrowing, he shook his head dismissively. 'I'm guessing you've never owned a motorbike.'

No, she had never even ridden a motorbike. They were noisy and dangerous: today was proof of that. And yet she couldn't help wondering what it would be like riding a bike *with him*. She could picture it perfectly— knew exactly how it would feel to lean into that broad back, to feel the bands of muscle tense against her as he shifted gear or leaned into a turn.

Her hands felt shaky, and suddenly it was difficult to breathe. Glancing over at his bike, and trying desperately to hang on to her indignation, she ignored the prickling heat rising over her collarbone. Just because it was new, it didn't mean he shouldn't pay attention to other road-users.

'No I haven't,' she agreed, her hands moving of their own accord to her hips, her brow creasing. 'But it wouldn't matter if I had. It still wouldn't change the fact that you should watch where you're going. This isn't a racetrack, you know.'

She frowned, her brain backtracking. How had he got into the estate anyway? The gates required a code. Maybe he'd wanted to show off his stupid bike to one of the staff, or perhaps he was picking someone up—either way it wasn't something she wanted to get involved in.

She glared at him. 'And you should be wearing a helmet.'

'Yes, I should,' he said softly, his green gaze resting on her face.

Something in his simple, uncompromising answer made her blood start to hum. She held her breath.

In the distance she could see the sea. So far she hadn't found anywhere on the estate where it wasn't possible to catch a glimpse of the unruffled turquoise water, and usually her eye sought it out. But today it was him, this man, who drew her gaze. Only why did he make her feel that way?

The situation—lone female on a deserted road with a strange man—should be making her feel uneasy, but she wasn't scared at all. Or not scared by *him* anyway, she thought, her cheeks suddenly hot as her eyes flitted hastily over the enticing curve of his mouth. The only threat was coming from her own imagination.

She felt another twitch of panic.

Her body was aching with a tension she didn't understand, and her hair, already hot and heavy in the early evening sun, felt as though it was crushing her skull, so that it was an effort to think straight.

Crossing her arms in front of her body, she forced herself to meet his eyes, and suddenly she was shaking again—only not with anger this time. There was something so intense in his gaze, so intimate…

Clearing her throat, she said quickly, 'Look, I don't have time for this. I need to get home.' And away from this intense man and the effect he had on her. Only… She glanced down the deserted road. 'But I suppose I can help you move your bike.'

'That won't be necessary.'

He stared at her calmly, and his calmness, his confidence, pulled her in so that her heart was slamming against her chest.

Only that was ridiculous—it was all ridiculous. Him and the effect he was having on her.

Wanting, needing, to escape the unsettling pull of tension between them, she took a step backwards, tightening her arms to contain the beat of heat pulsing in her chest.

'Fine. Suit yourself,' she said, sharpening her voice deliberately, pursing her lips in a disapproval she wanted to feel, but didn't. 'I get the feeling that's what you're best at anyway.'

'Excuse me?'

Now he turned, his eyes narrowing, and she felt a rush of satisfaction at having finally got under his skin.

'You heard me…' she began, but her words died in her throat, like an actor who had forgotten her lines, and breathing in sharply, her eyes dropped to the brilliant and distinctive red stain blooming on his shirtsleeve like a poppy opening to the sun.

Blood.

CHAPTER TWO

'YOU'RE BLEEDING!'

César Zayas y Diago gazed at the woman standing in front of him, frustration momentarily blotting out the pain in his arm. He didn't regret the injury. He never did. No matter how intense, physical pain was straight-forward and short-lived. It didn't make you question who you were.

'You're bleeding,' she said again.

She was English, not American—he recognised the accent—and a tourist, judging by her clothes. Probably she'd been sold a boat trip and then just dumped on the beach and left to find her own way home.

He would have to speak to his security team, but right now he needed to focus on the matter in hand—and most especially this titian-haired trespasser.

As his gaze fixed on her face his breath caught in his throat. *No wonder he'd gone head over heels.* She was astonishingly beautiful.

The first few seconds after coming off the bike he'd been too busy picking himself up to notice, his body distracted and tensed against any incoming pain. But now that he had time to look at her he was finding it hard not to stare.

She was slim, maybe too slim—certainly for his taste—but there were curves too beneath her clothes, and he could practically feel the heat coming off the cloud of flame-coloured hair that reached her elbows. But it was the contradiction between that accusatory, grey gaze and the sensual promise of that fascinating, perfect pink mouth that was making his head spin.

His shoulders tensed. Was it deliberate?

Somehow it seemed unlikely. His eyes flickered as-sessingly over her face. She looked nervous, less sure of herself than when she'd been berating him—or try-ing to berate him—in beginner's Spanish.

But then she'd just had a shock.

Glancing down at his right arm, he pressed his fin-gers against the damp fabric, grimacing.

This was supposed to have been a rare, unsched-uled moment of downtime. His day had started in Flor-ida. He'd woken early for a five-thirty session with his trainer and moved seamlessly into a four-hour meet-ing with his lawyers over some cheap import that was using almost identical bottle branding to Dos Rios. The email about the bike had come into his inbox just as the lawyers were leaving, and on impulse, he'd decided to take a diversion to Havana.

He still wasn't sure why he'd even ordered the bike in the first place. Coming to Cuba required both an effort of will and a secrecy he loathed but couldn't avoid—his parents got so upset when he returned home. But maybe, subconsciously, he'd just wanted to make a point to himself that he *could*.

Besides, a motorbike was an easy way to top up his need for adrenalin, a need that he recognised, and embraced in those hours not spent pursuing global domination of the rum market.

And it had felt good—not just the spontaneity of kicking free of his schedule, but the actual act of bonding with the bike. His body and mind had been immersed in the angles of the road and the rush of the wind—and then suddenly she was there.

Like all accidents, it had happened too quickly for him to have any real sense of anything beyond the bike slip-sliding away from him, the earth tilting on its axis, a glare of sunlight and a blur of trees, and then the noise of metal hitting stone, followed by silence.

Even before he'd looked down and seen the blood he'd known he'd hurt himself, but he'd had enough injuries to be able to differentiate between those requiring a Band-Aid and those that needed a trip to A&E. And anyway, after the first shock had worn off he'd been more worried about *her*.

She'd been so agitated and upset that he had deliberately angled his body away from hers so that she wouldn't see the blood—only then she'd fronted up to him, like a skinny little ginger cat, and he'd forgotten all about his arm.

Nothing had mattered except wiping that dismissive uppity sneer from her mouth.

Preferably with his mouth.

He felt his pulse jerk forward.

Careful, he warned himself. She might be beautiful, but he didn't need another lesson in the pitfalls of acting on impulse—and by that he didn't mean taking a bike for an unplanned road test.

Her eyes were wide with panic. 'Why didn't you say something?'

'It's fine.' He held up his hands placatingly, and then regretted it as a drop of blood splashed onto the pale dirt.

'How can you say that when you're dripping blood everywhere?'

She was looking at him as though she'd seen a ghost. For a moment he thought about telling her about the other times he'd come off a bike, but it might backfire and make her panic more. And anyway, it was private. All of it was private. His pursuit of precision, the transcendence of the everyday and that heightened awareness that came with being at one with the machine. How could he explain what it felt like to lose all sense of himself—his past, his position as CEO, all of it—in the heat and speed of the ride? Why would he want to explain that to her?

He glanced past her back down the empty road. Why was she even here? On her own. She was just a tourist and now she was in the middle of a drama. No wonder she looked out of her depth.

It made him feel both irritated and protective. And then he felt angry with himself for feeling anything at all. Feelings—his in particular—were dangerously unreliable. He had the scars to prove it. And he wasn't talking about the ones on his body.

'Look, nothing's broken. It's just a graze.'

'Even if it is you should still get it checked out. It's not worth taking the risk.'

His jaw tightened. It was on the tip of his tongue to tell her exactly who he was, and that this was his estate and she was trespassing, and therefore the risk was all hers. But that would only confuse matters further.

He raised an eyebrow. 'Is that a professional opinion?'

She glared at him, her chin jutting upwards. 'I don't have a car, but I could call an ambulance.'

An ambulance?

Frowning, he shook his head, contemplating all the time-consuming and unnecessary complications of such a step. 'Absolutely not. It can wait until I get home.'

Forehead creasing, she took a step forward. 'I don't think you should wait. What happens if you feel dizzy, or the bleeding won't stop?'

She hesitated, and he could see the conflict in her eyes—doubt at what she was about to suggest fighting with a determination to do the right thing. A long time ago he too had been just as transparent and easy to read. But he'd learnt the hard and humiliating way to keep his feelings hidden, or better still to avoid them altogether.

Her grey eyes rested on his face. 'Look, we can walk the bike back to my villa. It's not far from here. I have a first aid kit and I know how to clean a wound. At least let me take a look before you do anything else.'

So she lived nearby. He wondered where she was staying. From memory, he thought there were a couple of villas beyond the woods, but it seemed an odd place to choose as a holiday home. Most of Havana's visitors liked to be nearer the city centre and all the regular tourist attractions. But there was something about this woman that made him think that perhaps she wasn't here for the Malecón, the Gran Teatro or the Plaza Vieja.

So why was she here?

The answer shouldn't matter, but for some reason it did. Before he had a chance to wonder why, he heard himself say, 'Okay. You can take a look at it. But no ambulance.'

The walk to her villa took less than ten minutes.

Inside, she gestured towards a comfy-looking sofa. 'Sit down and I'll get you a glass of water.'

Sitting down, he felt a sense of *déjà-vu*. It was exactly the kind of traditional Cuban *cabaña* that his grandparents had grown up in, only theirs had been home to at least ten people. Not that they'd seemed to mind. For them—for his own parents too—family was everything.

He shifted in his seat, the ache in his chest suddenly sharper than the ache in his arm. He knew that his mother and father were proud of how he had built up the business, and grateful for the comfort and security he had given them, but what they really wanted—what would make them willingly give up their luxurious lifestyle in a heartbeat—was a grandchild they could spoil. Not that they said so, or at least his mother didn't, but he felt their hope every time he mentioned a woman's name in passing.

His stomach twisted. Children required parents, and typically that meant two people who loved one another, only that just wasn't going to happen for him. Maybe the right woman was out there somewhere, logically, statistically, he knew she must be. But no amount of logic could counteract the fact that he didn't trust himself to choose her, not after what had happened with Celia.

'Here.'

She was back. Handing him a glass, she sat down beside him with a bowl of water, a towel and a large plastic box. When she'd told him she had a first aid kit he'd assumed she meant something she'd picked up at the airport. This, though, looked on a par with the kits at the distillery.

'You're very well prepared,' he said softly.

He felt her tense.

'It's just the basics.' She glanced up at him accusingly. 'You should probably have a kit on your bike.'

In fact he did have one, and he was on the point of telling her that, but he was suddenly too distracted by the way her beautiful red-gold eyebrows were arching in concentration as she rummaged through the box.

Pulling out a packet, she looked up at him, her eyes meeting his, then dropping to the shining patch of crimson on his upper arm. 'I need to see if it's stopped bleeding.'

'Okay.' He nodded, but he was distracted by a glimpse of her feet. She had taken off her shoes, and there was something strangely arousing about her bare toes.

Pulling his gaze away, he glanced back up at her face.

A trace of pink coloured her cheeks. 'So I need you to take your shirt off,' she said huskily.

Kitty swallowed.

I need you to take your shirt off.

As her words reverberated inside her head and around the room her eyes darted towards the triangle of light gold skin at his throat. If only she'd just ignored his objections and called an ambulance. Outside, on the road, with his shirt turning red, she hadn't thought about anything but the fact that he needed help. She certainly hadn't envisaged him taking his clothes off. But how else was she going to be able to deal with his injury?

She cleared her throat. 'Or I could cut the sleeve off?' she offered.

He didn't reply. He just stared at her. And suddenly

she forgot all about his shirt, and even his injury, for nobody had ever looked at her so intently. It was as though he was trying to see inside her, to read her thoughts. Her muscles tightened against a sudden flood of heat. No one had ever looked at her with such focus, not even her husband. It was intimate, exhilarating, both an intrusion and a caress—

'No, it's fine. I'll take it off,' he said.

She watched as he started trying to undo the buttons, but they were sticky with blood, and before she knew what she was doing she leaned forward, batting his hands away.

'Here. Let me.'

Her heart began to beat faster as her fingers pulled at the buttons. She could feel the heat of him beneath his shirt and, try as she might, she couldn't stop her eyes from fixing on his sleek bronze skin as the fabric parted.

Her fingers twitched against the buckle of his belt and, avoiding his gaze, she lifted her hands and inched backwards. 'I'll let you take it from here,' she said.

He shrugged his left shoulder free and then peeled the shirt tentatively away from his injured arm.

For a moment she stared at him in silence, her heart pulsing in her throat. It had been such a long time since she had looked at a man's body. Or at least a body that looked like his.

With broad shoulders tapering to a slim waist his body was muscular, but not overly so, with just the finest trail of dark hair splitting the lean definition of his chest and stomach. His skin was smooth and golden, but it wasn't his skin that drew her gaze, but the two scars running almost parallel up his abdomen.

Clearly he hadn't been joking when he'd said he'd had far worse injuries. But why, having been so badly hurt, would anyone take more risks?

It wasn't a question she could ask a stranger—not even one sitting bare-chested on her sofa.

'What do you think?'

Lost in thought, she was caught unawares by his question and gazed up at him dazedly.

'What do I think?' she repeated his question slowly. Her brain seemed to have stopped working.

'About my arm.'

Dragging her eyes up to the curve of his bicep, she breathed out unsteadily. He had been right. The skin was scuffed, and crusted with grit from the road, but it was just a graze.

'I think it will be fine, but it'll be easier to say once I've cleaned it.' She gave him a small, tight smile. 'Tell me if I hurt you.'

There was quite a lot of blood, but she wasn't squeamish, not any more...not after everything she'd seen and had to do for Jimmy. And anyway it was easier not to think about what so nearly might have happened if there was something practical to do.

'I will.'

His eyes met hers and she felt his gaze flow over her skin, cool and dark and unfathomable like a woodland pool. Her stomach knotted fiercely. Outside, in the aftermath of the accident, there had been so much going on. Now, though, his aura was undiluted—a mix of sandalwood and sexual charisma that made a flicker of unfamiliar heat rise up inside her.

Forcing herself to ignore his body, she focused on trying to be as gentle as possible as she washed away the blood, carefully easing loose the tiny pieces of grit that were embedded in the graze. There was just one last bit now...

She could feel his pulse vibrating steadily beneath his skin, and yet one tiny variable on that road might have stopped it beating for ever. The thought made her shake inside with loss and anger—anger at the unfairness of life, and with this man who wore his beauty and certainty like a shield.

Biting her lip, she leaned in closer, resting her hand against his thigh to help steady herself.

'Sorry.' She'd heard him breathe in and, glancing up, saw he was gritting his teeth. 'Did I hurt you?'

She felt his leg muscle tighten, and quickly she lifted her hand.

'Not exactly,' he said, staring straight ahead. 'Have you finished?'

'Almost.' She patted his skin dry with the towel. 'I don't think it will bleed any more, but I'll put this dressing on, then you won't have to think about it.'

Glancing down, she frowned. 'Oh, I nearly forgot.' Picking up his hand, she washed the smudges of dried blood from his fingers. 'There.'

'Do you have children?'

'What?' She stared at him in confusion.

'I just thought—' He held her gaze. 'You just seem like someone who knows how to care for people, and you're so well-prepared.'

Her heart was pounding. It made no sense, but for one crazy moment she almost told him the truth. This man, this stranger. Only he didn't feel like a stranger. It felt like he knew her so well.

Throat tightening, she stared past him, remembering the months she and Jimmy had spent trying to get pregnant. She had so wanted to give him a baby, but her body just hadn't co-operated. By the time she'd decided to look into it medically, Jimmy had been diagnosed, and then afterwards it hadn't mattered anymore. Although, since arriving in Cuba her cycle had been all over the place, so clearly her body was just ultra-sensitive.

Lifting her chin, she found him looking at her. Meeting his gaze, she shook her head. 'No, I don't have any children. I can't have them,' she admitted.

Before, in England, it had always hurt even to think that sentence inside her head, but somehow saying it now, to him, made it hurt less. How crazy was that? And unfair. To her parents and friends and Lizzie. They had spent so long talking to her, and yet here she was opening up to this stranger—this semi-naked stranger.

Her face felt hot and tight. 'I'm sorry, you don't need to know that that.'

'Don't be sorry. I asked a question and you answered it.'

His words repeated themselves inside her head. He made it sound so simple. But of course it was simple. Everything was simple between them. They had no history, no past, no future. Nothing but a random connection on a dusty road.

And a fluttering pinwheel of anticipation spinning inside her stomach.

Had she been looking for love or seeking some kind of romantic adventure then it might have felt different. But there would never be anyone like Jimmy. What she'd felt for him had been unique, and it was over now—and that was fine, because she knew too how it felt to lose the one you loved, and she never wanted to feel that ache of loss again.

He shifted forward and her pulse boomeranged.

What she wanted now was *him*. This man. This nameless stranger. To feel the hot, languorous touch of his hands and lips warming her skin like sunshine.

His fingers brushed against hers and she tensed, her breath scraping against her throat.

She could smell his cologne, that hint of sandalwood and lemon, and beneath it his own clean, masculine scent, a sensual halo of salt and shade and burning sun. Her pulse leapt forward unsteadily, heat rising up over her throat as his dark green eyes rested on her face.

He was too close, but she couldn't move. She didn't want to move. She wanted to get closer, to touch the curve of his mouth, to feel the tension of his skin, the swell of his muscle. She wanted to hold him close, and be held, to have the warm, solid intimacy of his body pressing against hers.

'You're trembling.' He frowned. 'It's probably some kind of delayed shock. Let me get you—'

She felt suddenly desperate. Her blood pulsed against her skin. She didn't want him to leave. 'No.' Her fingers closed around his. 'No, it's not that.'

Her heart was suddenly beating too fast, and her blood felt as if it had turned to air.

For a second they both stared at each other. He was so close now—close enough that she could feel the heat of his skin and see the flecks of amber in his eyes.

He wasn't a memory or a fantasy.

He was beautiful, full of life and energy, warm and solid and real.

And he was shaking too. She could feel him.

The sound of her heartbeat was filling her head. She felt almost dizzy with longing.

'No, it's not that,' she said again. 'It's this...'

Leaning forward, she pressed her hand against his chest and breathed out unevenly. His skin was warm and smooth and taut, just as she'd imagined. And beneath it she could feel his heart hammering in time with hers.

He sucked in a breath, his jaw tightening. In his narrowed eyes she could see desire fighting with control, and she felt her breath dissolve as he reached up and stroked her cheek.

For a moment their eyes locked, and they breathed each other in, and then, leaning forward, she brushed her lips hesitantly against his, her mouth clumsy with the freedom of touching him.

'I don't even know your name...' he whispered against her mouth.

'It doesn't matter.'

She kissed him again and he pulled back a little, his fierce green gaze trained on her face. She knew that he was giving her space to think, time to change her mind.

Her heart was racing. Should she say something? Tell him that this wasn't who she was ordinarily? That she'd changed her mind. Only she couldn't say that because it would be a lie.

And it would mean stopping, and she didn't want to stop. She didn't want to think or speak or explain. She just wanted to lose herself in this moment, lose herself in him, because right now this *was* what she was, and he was who she wanted.

Threading her fingers through his hair, she pulled him closer. Instantly he pulled her closer too, angling his body, his tongue, to deepen the kiss. His hands slid beneath her blouse, moving over her back from her hip to her waist, up to the catch of her bra.

He stripped her out of her clothing and pulled her onto his lap so that she was straddling him. Lowering his mouth, he kissed her breast, brushing his lips against one nipple and then the other, and in a heartbeat her body turned to liquid.

The intensity of her desire was both a shock and a revelation. Always before it had been a slow and steady progress. This was like throwing a match on gasoline— a pure white-hot blazing urgency that blotted out everything but a need for more.

His hands were at her waist, pulling her down. His mouth was seeking hers now, and instinctively she reached for his buckle.

Groaning, he grabbed her wrists. 'Let's go to your room.' He was fighting to get the words out.

'No.' Tugging her hands free, she pulled the belt open, and then the zip, and felt his body tense as her fingers wrapped around him.

He groaned again, his hands stilling hers. 'I don't have any condoms.'

'I don't either.'

For a moment, she was shocked. In the heat of everything, she had forgotten. But his words reassured her, for clearly he was a responsible lover, and the fact that he was holding back made her feel that she could trust him.

'It's okay.' Leaning forward, she looped her arms around his neck and kissed him fiercely.

Groaning, he raised his hips, shrugging himself free of his trousers, and then he leaned backwards, taking her with him.

His pupils flared and for a second she rode him lightly, teasing the hard, straining length of him, revelling in her power to arouse him. And then, gripping his shoulders for balance, she parted her legs and guided him inside her.

He breathed in sharply. His jaw was taut with concentration, the muscles in his arms and chest bunching as she began to rock back and forth, her breath quickening in her throat as his fingers moved between her thighs, working in time to the fervent, pulsing ache there.

His eyes locked on hers—dark, rapt, blazing. '*Mírame!* Look at me,' he said, his voice hoarse.

She was fighting for control. Heat was gathering inside her and she clutched frantically at his arms, pulling him closer and then pushing him away, needing to let go but wanting to make it last for ever.

Her muscles clenched, her breathless body gripping his. She felt his hands catch in her hair and suddenly she couldn't bear it any longer. Arching against him, she tensed against the heat and the hardness, shuddering helplessly. He groaned, pushing against her, seeking more depth, and then, gasping into her mouth, he thrust upwards.

CHAPTER THREE

SLOWLY CÉSAR BREATHED OUT, his eyes blinking open. For a moment he didn't know where he was—and then he remembered. He must have fallen asleep for a moment, lulled by the languid warmth of her body and the sudden heaviness of his own limbs.

Fixing his eyes on the ceiling, he frowned. It had been a long time since he had held a woman close like this, more than a decade, at least. But then today had been exceptional for any number of reasons.

His chest tightened as he felt the most exceptional of those reasons shift beside him.

Glancing down at her naked body curled around his, he felt his pulse accelerate. He'd just done the one thing he'd sworn never to do again—he'd let his libido dictate his actions.

He grimaced. As if he needed any reminding about the consequences of that youthful, humiliating indiscretion. They were branded in his conscience and he could still feel his parents' shock and disappointment across the years. After he'd made such a fool of himself with Celia he'd sworn never to let a woman get under his skin. And he'd kept his promise.

Until today.

Until...

He gritted his teeth. *Maldita sea!* Thanks to his sudden and completely uncharacteristic loss of self-control he didn't even know her name, but the strength and speed of his desire had caught him unawares. He should have fobbed her off on the road. Better still, he should have called Andreas, his head of security, and let him deal with her. It was his job, after all. But instead he'd let himself be distracted by a curving pink mouth.

He could have called a halt when she'd leaned forward and kissed him with that same perfect, pink mouth, but as her lips had melted against his, his brain, his body, his self-control had gone into meltdown. His past, his promises had been forgotten. Nothing had mattered but her. His whole being had been fixed on the need to touch and taste every inch of her, and even now his still-hungry body was clamouring for more.

But perfect pink lips could still lie and deceive and frankly there was no need for him to go there again. He might have been young, but he was a quick learner—and that lesson had been well and truly drummed into him.

His mouth twisted. So what now?

As though she could hear his thoughts, the woman shifted against him, and instantly his groin began to ache. Reluctant to reveal the hard proof of her ability to turn him on, he started to move. But she was already inching backwards, peeling her damp skin away from his and scooping up the muddle of clothes from the floor in one graceful movement.

Was she practised at this?

The thought snagged in his head and then he pushed

it quickly away. It was none of his business, and besides he wasn't in any position to judge.

'Here,' she murmured. 'These are yours.'

Looking up, he gritted his teeth.

She was pulling her blouse over her head and, catching a glimpse of her pale, curving breast, he felt his skin twitch, his body hardening and aching with a sudden, sharp, serrated hunger. She looked impossibly sexy, and suddenly the heated, passion-filled minutes of earlier felt like just a taster before the main meal.

He wanted more. He wanted to feel that soft skin next to his and the whisper of her breath against his mouth.

He felt another twitch of desire—although this time it might just as easily have been irritation.

Obviously he wanted more.

His last 'relationship' had ended a little over seven weeks ago and, having been flat out at work ever since, trying to resolve this damned trademark dispute, he'd neglected his personal life. Although, given how hard he tried to maintain boundaries, maybe *im*personal life might be a better description.

Either way, to put it bluntly he hadn't had sex in a long time, and this beautiful, uninhibited woman standing in front of him had stirred his hunger.

So what if she had?

It had happened, and it had been incredible. Better than incredible, he thought, his heartbeat jerking as their tangle on the sofa replayed inside his head. And he wasn't going to pretend that he wouldn't willingly pull her back onto that sofa and carry on where they'd left off. Or deny that she was attractive, or that he was attracted to her. But whatever this was—this thing he was feeling, this unruly, insistent enchantment that had sneaked up on him unannounced—he wasn't going to act on it again, no matter how hollowed out with longing he felt.

In fact, his unprecedented physical response only increased his determination to stay cool and detached. For he'd already made the mistake of trusting his body before, and his libido had been proved a poor judge of character.

He glanced down at the scars that ran across his chest and down his muscled abdomen. They might come from a different kind of foolhardy behaviour, but they were honestly acquired, and not the result of emotional weakness or self-delusion.

There would be other women, and next time he would look where he was going.

A breath of cool air drifted over his skin and, leaning forward, he took his trousers and shirt from her outstretched hand and started to get dressed.

In his experience, women normally tried to extend this moment. It was one of the reasons he always preferred to find somewhere neutral to meet. But this woman hadn't even wanted to know his name, and having sex with him didn't appear to have changed that fact.

It was a completely new experience for him—one that in theory he should welcome. And yet he found himself feeling slightly aggrieved by her lack of curiosity.

But then in some ways—although he wouldn't make a habit of it—his anonymity, and hers, was actually a bonus. For the first time in his life he'd had sex with a woman who didn't know or care who he was and, weirdly, he found himself trusting her more because of that.

This hadn't been some carefully planned attempt to seduce him. Nothing was fake. She hadn't told him she loved him or that he was special, nor made any promises. They had both got what they wanted and now they could get back to their lives.

He buckled up his belt and began pulling on his shirt, ignoring the slight tightness in his arm as he pushed it into the sleeve.

'Is your arm okay?'

Looking up, he felt his pulse slow. A lock of that glorious red hair hung loosely across her forehead, and he had to stop himself from reaching out and smoothing it away from her face.

'Yes. Good as new.'

Holding his gaze, she gave him a small stiff smile. 'I'm glad.'

There was a moment of silence, and then she cleared her throat. 'Look, I don't really know what's normal for this situation. I don't usually do this kind of thing, you know—'

He waited a moment, then shrugged. 'Me neither.'

Watching the tic of tension along the curve of her jaw, he knew for certain that he'd got under her skin. What was less certain, though, was why that mattered to him.

She flushed. 'Okay, well… I'm sure you've got things to be getting on with.'

His hand stilled against the top button of his shirt. In other words she wanted him to leave. She was kicking him out.

'Of course.' He felt a twist of irritation, followed by a sudden intense need to dictate the terms of their encounter. Deliberately slowing down the buttoning of his shirt, he glanced assessingly round the room. 'Nice house,' he said slowly. 'How did you find it?'

Her eyes met his. 'It came with my job.'

He felt a ripple of disquiet. 'What job?'

She frowned, not at his question but at the terseness in his voice that he hadn't bothered to disguise.

'I work for Dos Rios—you know, the rum. You might have heard of them.'

His chest tightened. Dos Rios had a policy of providing temporary accommodation for consultants and overseas contractors. His PA would know the details, but obviously he wouldn't have been notified. The comings and goings of his employees was way below his pay grade.

'I should do,' he said. 'As the business was founded by my family.'

He paused, watching her face as he let his words sink in.

'What do you mean?'

The colour had drained from her cheeks. She was staring at him in confusion.

'I—I didn't— I don't…' She was struggling to speak.

'Understand?' He finished her sentence. 'Then perhaps I should introduce myself. My name is César Zayas y Diago.'

In the still, tense silence that followed his remark, Kitty felt her insides loosen. 'No, you can't be,' she said hoarsely.

Her stomach was in freefall.

It couldn't be him. It *couldn't* be, she thought frantically. She'd been in the labs only yesterday, and surely somebody would have said something about his imminent arrival.

He must be lying.

Only her skin felt suddenly too tight, her heartbeat too loud, and as though she was looking at him for the first time she registered the tiny pleats at the top of his shirtsleeves; the expensive dark suit trousers and the handmade black leather brogues.

His eyes rested on her face and she felt a prickle of heat spread over her skin as he held out his hand.

'I assure you I am.'

His voice had grown cooler, its authority no longer like quicksilver beneath the surface but smooth and inflexible like high tensile steel, and with a pang of acceptance she knew that he was telling the truth.

There was only one thing to do and, feeling her breath ricocheting against her ribs, she took his hand and shook it briefly.

His eyes raked her face and then he smiled. Only it wasn't the slow, languorous smile of her imagination. Instead it was cool and assessing and uncompromising. The smile of a CEO...the smile of a boss.

Her boss.

Her heart was leaping against her ribs. Surely there was some mistake? But she knew that there wasn't. No matter which way she turned, the picture and the facts were still the same.

She'd just had sex—wild, unplanned sex—on a sofa with the man who signed her paycheque.

Her head was spinning.

In the five years since Jimmy's death she'd not so much as looked at a man—she certainly hadn't been intending to meet one today. Ironically, if she had been, she would have been taking more care and she might not have stepped out in front of his bike.

But out there on the road there had been more going on than just a near accident. They might not have collided physically, but some invisible chemical reaction had been set in motion.

Her pulse pitched, carried along by another current of panic.

If he'd simply summoned her into his office and introduced himself, like any normal boss, this would never have happened. But, no, he'd had to fall off his motorbike, so she'd had all those unnecessary and confusing and *unguarded* emotions churning around inside her. And that tension between them had kept on winding tighter and tighter.

Remembering the feel of his body against hers, she felt heat wrap around her face. With him she had become another person. His hands, his mouth, had unlocked a wildly passionate woman. Her hunger had been beyond her control—she hadn't known it was possible to feel what he'd made her feel. It had been incredible, and she was still reeling from what had happened. And the fact that she had made it happen.

She had wanted that tumult of touch and release. She had wanted the solid weight of a man's body pressing into her. She had wanted him.

Not love or commitment. Not a future or a soulmate. She knew the void in her heart would never, *could* never, be filled by any man, because she knew the other side of love was loss, and she simply didn't have it in her to deal with that terrible ache of loneliness.

After Jimmy had died the pain had been unbearable, and she'd sworn never to allow herself to be that vulnerable again. It was easier simply to shut down that part of her life rather than risk having it snatched away again.

But she was still a woman, and this man was so gorgeous, and suddenly that had been enough. Enough for her to let go, to let her hair down. Only now she understood that a part of why it had been enough had been their anonymity and the knowledge that she would never have to see him again.

And now it turned out that she was working for him.

She looked up at him, dazed and then out of nowhere she pictured her sister's face. Lizzie wouldn't care that César was her boss. She would argue that desire was a great equaliser. Of course that was hard to do when your skin was still humming from the heat and hardness of your boss's body, but she couldn't change what had happened so she was just going to have to face it head-on.

Her stomach clenched. And becoming a widow had taught her all she needed to know about facing difficulties head-on. 'I didn't know who you were.'

His eyes found hers. 'Clearly. Unless you always try to kill your boss and then seduce him.'

Her cheeks felt suddenly hot. 'I didn't try and kill you. You nearly ran me over.'

He stared at her impassively. 'But you did seduce me.'

She felt her stomach knot. It wasn't a question, and there was no point in lying. 'If I'd known who you were—'

He raised an eyebrow. 'So you work for me?'

'I work for Dos Rios.'

After what had just happened between the two of them it seemed important to differentiate between the man and his business.

The slight curl to his lip suggested that he registered her intent. 'In what capacity?'

'I'm working on the anniversary rums,' she said quickly. 'I'm Kitty Quested.'

They'd already shaken hands, so instead she forced her mouth into a small, stiff smile. Out of the corner of her eye she caught a glimpse of the corner of the sofa, and her pulse moonwalked backwards. This polite formality after the fierce intimacy of earlier felt horribly artificial and unsettling.

Looking up, she met his gaze. He smiled—the kind of smile that made it difficult to swallow.

'I remember,' he said slowly. 'Blackstrap.'

The word echoed like a gunshot around the quiet room. She felt a ripple of panic. He was going to sack her. 'I know what you're thinking...'

'And I know what you're thinking.' He held her gaze. 'But, no, I'm not going to fire you. And, yes, with hindsight, that—' he gestured towards the sofa '—was probably a bad idea, but it's too late to worry about that now.'

He paused, and she felt her face grow warm as his dark green eyes dropped to her mouth.

'In fact it was too late way back when I saw you out there on the road.'

Her breath caught in her throat. She felt her body stirring, and then a swift rush of shame. How could she have such a strong response to a man who, to be frank, she hardly knew? When the man she'd loved, and still loved, was dead. It made no sense, and it was going to stop now.

Whatever connection they had, it would be better, simpler, safer if it existed solely on a professional basis from now on.

'This won't happen again. Obviously.' She spoke in a rush, needing to know that he understood and felt the same way as she did. 'It was just...' She searched for the word.

'Sex?' he suggested.

Her cheeks were growing pinker, but she held his gaze. 'Yes, it was just sex, and what's more important is our working relationship, so I think it would be best if we just put it all behind us.'

He stared at her in silence. Then, 'That won't be a problem,' he said softly. 'From now on you and I have a clean slate. But you don't need to worry about our working relationship, Ms Quested. I really don't spend much time in Havana.'

His words were clipped, his expression impassive.

'Enjoy your time at Dos Rios and I wish you luck in the rest of your career.'

She watched as he turned and walked quickly across the room. As the door closed behind him, she breathed out unsteadily.

He was gone, and that was what she wanted.

Better still, it sounded as though there would be no chance of them ever meeting again, and that was what she wanted too.

It was better that way. Her throat tightened.

All she needed to do now was make herself believe it.

CHAPTER FOUR

HUNCHING OVER THE screen of her laptop, Kitty stared despondently at her notes. She was trying not to panic but there was no point in denying the obvious: after weeks of trial and experimentation, she was stuck.

Straightening her spine, she gazed around the space-age Dos Rios labs, breathing unsteadily, suddenly ridiculously close to tears.

She hardly ever cried. In books and films tears could cure blindness and mend wounds. In real life, though, they just gave you a headache and made your skin all blotchy.

But for the last few weeks she'd kept feeling this sadness. Not like the grief of losing Jimmy—a grief that had made her feel as if she was at the bottom of the ocean, gazing up through black waters. This feeling was nothing like that. It was just frustration that she couldn't seem to do her job.

It didn't help that at Blackstrap the creative process had felt so organic and effortless.

Partly that had been down to the fact that the business had only just been starting up, so there had been no actual deadline and therefore no pressure. And, of course, Bill was so incredibly laid-back.

Now, though, she was working for a global brand that had become almost a byword for rum, and time was running out.

Thinking of Jimmy, and their short, sweet marriage, she felt a lump rise in her throat. She knew all about time running out.

But she was not going to go there and, pushing her memories aside, she closed her laptop and slid it into her bag. She took the stairs down to the foyer and stepped out into the sunlight. After the chilled air of the labs the heat felt like an oven, and she was grateful to get into the air-conditioned cool of the car that took her to and from work.

Leaning back, she closed her eyes. Probably part of the reason she felt so defeated was that she was tired, the kind of tired that felt like an actual weight, physically crushing her.

She sighed. It was her own fault. She'd been sleeping badly and waking early and, although she'd grown used to her own company, the days had started to feel very long. So, without planning it, she'd fallen into a routine of going into the labs and staying late.

Clearly she was in a rut. She needed to forget about rum, put on some sunscreen and get some exercise and fresh air. She couldn't remember the feeling of sunshine on her face—and when had she last gone for a walk?

Her pulse stilled. Oh, she knew exactly when she'd last gone for a walk. It was not something she was likely to forget—or rather he was *someone* she was not likely to forget.

Picturing César Zayas's green-eyed gaze and his hard, muscular body, she felt her skin tighten, and she pressed her thighs together, her muscles tensing against a sudden, dizzying flood of heat.

She had promised herself that she wasn't going to think about him today. It was the same promise she'd made and failed to keep every day since he'd walked out of her villa.

Her cheeks felt hot. It had been stupid to feel that way when he'd been a complete stranger, but it was even more stupid, not to say baffling and pointless, to feel that way now she knew he was her boss.

Only she just couldn't stop herself thinking about his beautiful, masculine face, about his hands and his mouth, and the hard, insistent pressure of his body against hers.

But it was going to stop.

Not because she regretted what had happened. She didn't. It had been amazing. But whatever her feelings had been, they had nothing to do with any kind of reality. Things had just got a little out of hand...

Trembling, she opened her eyes and gazed out of the window at the broad fields of sugarcane.

It was obviously not ideal, him being her boss and everything, but she knew why it had happened. After Jimmy had died she'd stopped eating. Not deliberately—she'd just seemed to forget about food. All she'd wanted to do was sleep. Eventually, over time, her appetite had come back, and even though she was still a little on the slim side her weight was perfectly normal now.

What wasn't normal, though—or healthy—was being celibate for so long.

And it wasn't just sex. Aside from sharing hugs with her family, she now lived a life bereft of physical contact. She didn't even have a pet—a cat or a dog she could cuddle.

She was twenty-seven years old and it had been five years since she'd kissed or been kissed. So she'd wanted to remember what it felt like to have a man pull her close, to feel his warm hands and lips on her skin. Maybe if she'd given in to that need earlier then she wouldn't be feeling like this now, but after years of virtually ignoring an entire gender, was it any surprise that she'd been knocked sideways by that moment of wild, feverish passion that had flared between the two of them?

Back at the villa, she had a long, cool shower, using her favourite body wash, and then sat down on her bed with a book and a glass of mango juice. Normally she hated fruit juice, but for some reason she'd suddenly started craving it.

Twenty minutes later, she hadn't read a word, and she still hadn't shifted the heaviness in her limbs.

She knew it was psychosomatic…that if she managed to find that elusive inspiration everything would change in a heartbeat. Her mood would lighten and she would finally be able to blank her mind to the memory of her mysterious too-attractive boss, and that fierce, involuntary pull of attraction she had felt for him.

If only she could find those elusive notes that would make the rum sing. But nothing she'd tried was working.

She felt another prickle of panic and then, as she glanced across the room, she noticed the dress hanging from the handle of her wardrobe.

It had been an impulse buy.

In the weeks leading up to her flight to Cuba she'd

gone on a shopping trip to London, mainly to shut Lizzie up. Knowing that her sister would be appalled if she came home with nothing but insect repellent and a hat, she'd gone into one of those boutiques where even a basic T-shirt cost as much as her train fare home. Feeling horribly provincial and out of place, she been rummaging through a rail of linen cardigans, trying to look as though she was a regular customer, and there it had been.

Shocking pink, with a riotous pattern of exotic-looking flowers, it had tiny cap sleeves and a flippy little skirt that showed off her legs. It was bright, sexy and eye-wateringly expensive—in short, absolutely not the kind of dress she would ever normally buy. But in her head it had seemed to fit perfectly with her fantasy of a crowded Havana nightclub filled with beautiful dancing couples.

And suddenly, with a dawn-breaking kind of clarity, she knew what she was going to do.

She was going to go out in Havana. She was going to drink mojitos and dance and follow the pulsing salsa rhythm right to the heart of Cuba.

'I'm sorry, Señor Zayas, but the road ahead is closed so I'm going to have to go through the centre.'

Looking up from his laptop, César gazed out of the window of his SUV to where a queue of cars were jostling for position, accompanied by an escalating cacophony of horns and shouts.

He frowned at his driver. 'Is it an accident?'

'I don't think so, sir. It looks like roadworks.'

'It's fine, Rodolfo,' he said. 'I can wait.'

His shoulders stiffened. If that was true, then why

had he turned his entire schedule on its head and ordered Miguel, his pilot, to divert mid-flight to Havana instead of going to the Bahamas as planned?

He was in the process of buying a new catamaran, and had been on his way to Freeport to meet with the architects and the marine engineers when he'd changed his mind. Or that was what he'd told himself and his bemused air crew. The truth was that he'd pretty much been returning to Havana ever since he'd walked out of that villa on his estate seven weeks ago, his blood humming in his veins, his body reeling.

He felt his gut tighten.

Kitty Quested.

For the first few days after leaving Havana he'd resisted pulling her file, but finally he'd relented, assuming that if he answered the questions buzzing round his head the mystery would be solved. Instead, though, his questions had multiplied.

She was younger than he'd realised, and professionally inexperienced. How, then, had she created such an outstanding rum?

Creating such nuanced, complex flavours would have taken patience and persistence—qualities that were rare at that age. *He* certainly hadn't had them when his father had sat him down and told him that it was time to step up and take over the running of Dos Rios.

He felt his chest tighten, remembering his reaction at the time. Shock and disbelief—and then panic. He hadn't been ready, not nearly ready, to do what his father had asked of him. An indulged childhood had been no preparation for the responsibilities involved in running the family business. And after finishing his degree he'd wanted to travel, not work. To have fun, and to be free of his parents' unconditional and sometimes stifling love.

He couldn't blame them for wanting to be so involved in his life. They'd wished and waited for a baby so long, suffered so many disappointments. By the time he was born it had been too late for there to be any brother or sister and his fate had been sealed. He would always be unique, cherished and beloved.

He knew he was incredibly lucky to be so wanted, but his position as their only son and heir was complicated. For years he had prayed for a sibling. Not because he'd been lonely, nor even because he had known it would make his parents happy, but just so he wouldn't have to be so exceptional.

His prayers had gone unanswered, but—incredibly—his parents had agreed to give him a year after graduating from his MBA. A year to make his way alone in the world and make his own mistakes. And that was exactly what he'd done.

And look how that turned out.

He had ended up hurting the ones who loved him the most. The only consolation in the whole sorry mess was that it had taught him a valuable life lesson: that trust was something to be earned, not given.

And yet, incomprehensibly, he had felt as though he could trust Kitty.

But then nothing made sense about that woman. From her sudden appearance on the deserted road to that tantalising passion she'd revealed in that darkening villa.

She was a mystery, an enigma, with a glorious riot of red hair, a pale, serious face and mesmerisingly expressive grey eyes that switched in a flash from concern to fury.

Was it any wonder that for weeks now she had been popping into his head without invitation but with maddening regularity?

Images of her beautiful naked body undulating against his, the last shreds of sunlight spilling across their damp, feverish skin, had hounded his days and haunted his dreams, so that for the first time since adolescence his body had been at the mercy of his hormones.

And so he'd come back to Havana.

For years now he'd rationed his visits—more so since he'd moved his parents to live in Palm Beach—and on arrival he instantly felt that familiar sense of conflict. Relief at being home fighting with regret that he could never truly be himself here. But that was the way it had to be. The open, easy-going young man who had left Cuba to go to college in the States had never returned. Instead, in his place was a man who lived a life of order and restraint.

He gritted his teeth. Most of the time anyway.

That *rollo* with Kitty Quested shouldn't have happened. Normally he was so careful, so considered, plus she was an employee. But something had started out on that road…a spark had been struck.

His muscles tensed as he remembered. Not the impact of metal hitting gravel, but the moment when he'd looked up and she had been running towards him, that incredible red hair flying behind her like a comet's tail. She'd looked so small and fragile, but she had been moving with the same fierce determination as the waves that rode in to La Setenta beach.

He'd felt her panicky fear, had seen it too, for she'd been shaking. Only then she'd started scolding him, and he'd realised that it wasn't fear but anger, and all at once he'd been angry with her for lecturing him and being so impossibly, maddeningly righteous.

But mainly for having that incredible enticingly pink mouth.

And suddenly they had both been shaking. Only not with anger.

Replaying the moment again inside his head, he frowned. At the time there had been so much going on, but of course there was a perfectly logical explanation for that strange weave of tension.

Feelings had been running high.

An accident, anger, and confusion over their respective identities had obviously acted like emotional gunpowder, and his own spiking adrenaline was the spark which had ignited that intense, reluctant attraction he'd felt.

An attraction that he'd confidently expected to fade by the time he walked out of her villa.

Only he'd been wrong.

And that was why he needed to see her again.

His fingers twitched against the keyboard.

Last time he'd had no choice but to leave—to flee, really. Not just from Kitty, but from the past that haunted him, from a weakness he had thought he could only escape by keeping himself away from temptation.

And she had been a temptation. More than that, she had been a compulsion, and he'd been shocked and scared to discover that he still had that same weakness inside him—the weakness that had caused him and his family so much pain.

He'd had no choice. In Cuba, with her so tantalisingly close, there would have been a chance that he might give in to temptation. Clearly he'd needed to put some distance between the two of them—not just to remove the risk of that happening but to get his head in order.

Only that hadn't happened. He'd flown to Florida, then to New York and across to San Francisco. But all those thousands of miles had made no difference. She had got inside his head so that he couldn't think about anything other than her, and it was then that he'd realised that he'd made a mistake.

By leaving so swiftly he'd basically gone 'cold turkey'. His body was suffering withdrawal symptoms. He wanted more, and he was denying himself. Worse, he'd turned her into some kind of forbidden fruit—an illicit, off-limits pleasure—so of course he hadn't been able to stop thinking about her.

Seeing her again would make her real and attainable, and her power over him would simply disappear. Then he would take a new lover, someone who neither worked for him nor lived on his doorstep, and his hunger for this red-haired Englishwoman would be forgotten. Kitty Quested would be just a name on a payslip.

Feeling calmer, he settled back against his seat. The sky was beginning to turn pink and the brash, modern hotels were giving way to grand palm-filled squares and roads crammed with *almendróns*—iconic vintage American cars in a mouthwatering array of pick-'n'-mix colours. The SUV slowed, bumping over the cobbled streets of the Habana Vieja, and he leaned forward, his gaze drawn to the view outside the window.

It was a typical Friday night in his hometown. The streets seemed to swell with noise and laughter, and everywhere there were people. Beautiful, smiling people, chatting, dancing, holding up their phones to take photos. He scanned their faces, remembering how it had felt to be that carefree, so unquestioning of his right to happiness.

And then his gaze snagged on something teasingly familiar.

Hair the colour of damp beech leaves and the curve of a cheekbone, pale and luminous in the fading light.

He frowned. It couldn't be. Not in that dress. Or those heels.

But then she turned and he felt shock break over him like a wave. *It was her.* He watched as Kitty nodded to the dark-haired woman following her, her lips parting in a smile that made his vision go watery at the edges, and then, turning, she ran as lightly as a dancer up the steps into a bar.

It took his brain approximately ten seconds to go from mute disbelief to a memory of her as she had been that evening, arching against him, the curve of her back beneath his hand—

His shock was forgotten and instead he was tensing, his body reduced to nothing more than a swirling mass of instincts and hormones.

'Stop the car.'

'I'm sorry, sir?'

He heard the surprise in Rodolfo's voice but ignored it. 'Just pull over.'

'Yes, sir.'

Feeling the car slow, his heartbeat accelerated.

'I just need to speak to someone,' he said. 'Take the car round the block and I'll call you when I need to be picked up.'

Without waiting to hear his driver's reply he opened the car door and stepped out onto the pavement. The air was sweet and humid, tinged with cigarette smoke, and behind the buzz of chatter and laughter he could hear bursts of reggaeton and salsa from the nearby bars. But he barely registered anything other than the bright yellow door through which Kitty had just disappeared.

He glanced at the sign. *Bar Mango*. He didn't know it, but he didn't need to. He could picture exactly what it would be like: the heat, the hormones pulsing in time to the sound system…the heaving crush of strangers acting like lovers.

Moving quickly through the crowds, he took the steps two at a time, sidestepping a group of American tourists and pushing open the door. Inside the bar the music was deafening and the temperature was several degrees higher than on the street. The room was jammed with people shouting to one another.

'*Oye, asere, qué hacemos hoy?*'

'*Qué vola, hermano?*'

He surveyed the crowd, feeling his heart beating exponentially faster as each dimly lit corner failed to reveal her. Surely she couldn't have left already?

His shoulders tensed against an unreasonable rush of disappointment—and then tensed again as suddenly he saw her.

A pinwheel of relief spun inside his chest as he wondered how he had missed her. She was standing next to the bar, talking to the same dark-haired woman he'd seen before, and clearly they were part of a larger group of girls, all about the same age as Kitty—*chicas*, his mother would have called them.

They were all young, beautiful, and confident in

their vivid, lustrous beauty, but he could feel them fading away as he continued to stare at Kitty. She seemed to glow in the darkness, her glossy hair and mouth, the contours of her cheekbones a masterclass in chiaroscuro.

The word whispered against his skin, and he felt his body reacting both to the seductive lure of the syllables and the association in his mind between shadows and silence—and sex.

He breathed out unsteadily.

In another life, with any other woman, he might have hesitated, but watching her lean in closer to the barman, and the man's flirtatious smile, he felt his heart throb in his throat—and then he was shouldering a path through the sweaty, shifting tangle of bodies.

He had no idea what he was going to say, much less how she would react to seeing him there, but there was no time to worry about the unknown. For, as though sensing the gap opening up behind her, Kitty turned away from the smiling barman and glanced over her shoulder.

'Señor Zayas?'

Her grey eyes widened and he felt a swell of excitement as her gaze collided with his. He glanced at her, his spine tensing as it had on the bike just before he lost control. This time, however, it was her, and not the ground, that was causing his body to brace for impact.

'Ms Quested.'

It sounded so formal, so completely at odds with the way he'd been thinking about her just moments earlier, that suddenly he was struggling to find words. His one consolation was that she seemed more dazed and taken aback than he was.

Cheeks flushing, she stared at him uncertainly. 'I didn't know you were back.'

He found her confusion and the blush that accompanied it oddly satisfying. Back in control, he held her gaze. 'I arrived this evening.' Over her shoulder, he could see a trio of women glancing over at him. 'Are you out with friends?'

'Yes.' She hesitated. 'Actually, I met them for the first time tonight. There's an online group for expats. I got in touch and we arranged to get together this evening.'

Her eyes met his and her expression was—what? Defiant? Scared? Tense? Determined?

'How about you? Are you with friends?'

For a moment he thought about telling the truth— how she had got under his skin in a way that he didn't understand, or like, but that he couldn't seem to resist, so that when he'd seen her on the street he'd been compelled to follow her.

And then his brain caught up with his body, and he nodded. 'I've just left them,' he lied. 'I noticed you come in, so I thought I'd come and...you know...say hello.' His body twitched. 'Introduce myself properly.'

Beneath the throb of the music he felt something pulse between them, and he knew from the flare of response in her eyes that she had felt it too.

'About what happened—' she began.

'Kitty? We're thinking of going down the street to Candela. It's another bar, but not so quiet, you know? Is that okay?' Glancing up at him, the dark-haired woman feigned surprise, her mouth curving upwards. 'Sorry, I didn't mean to interrupt.'

'Oh, you're not.' Kitty said. 'Carrie, this is...' she hesitated.

'César.' He finished her sentence smoothly, keeping his voice casual.

'Nice to meet you, César.' Carrie smiled. 'So how do you two know each other?'

Kitty looked startled. 'Oh, we—we're—'

'Friends. We met through work.' He smiled at Carrie. 'Are you from England too?'

Carrie nodded. 'London. Look, you're welcome to join us—' she flicked a glance at Kitty '—but I'll leave you two to talk it over.' She gave Kitty's arm a quick squeeze. 'Just let me know what you want to do, okay?'

As Kitty nodded the crowd pushed forward and she was driven into him by the tide-swell of people, and fleetingly her soft curves were pressed against his groin. His mind blanked but he reacted instinctively, grabbing her elbow to steady her.

Watching her pupils flare, a buzz went through his body like the trembling of an electric storm. Not wanting to reveal his instant uncensored response to her sudden proximity, he let her go and took a step backwards, using his arm to create a space.

'Sorry.'

'It's not your fault—it's crazy in here.' She glanced across the crowded room. 'Is this really a *quiet* bar?'

He laughed. They were both having to shout to be heard. 'For Cuba, yes.'

She smiled, and then her smile stiffened. 'Why did you say we're friends? We're not friends.'

He held her gaze. 'We're not exactly strangers either.'

Her cheeks darkened. 'About that—' She glanced away, then back to his face. 'It shouldn't have happened.'

'Why shouldn't it? We're both grown-ups. And single.'

It wasn't a question, but his stomach tensed as he

watched her small upturned face brace against his words, and then she nodded and he felt his body loosen.

'I know, but I work for you.'

'You work for Dos Rios.'

Recognising her own words, she gave him another small smile and then looked away. 'I just want us to have a professional working relationship, and I know you said that wouldn't be a problem.'

'It's not.' Suddenly, fiercely, he wanted her to trust him. 'And it won't be.'

He knew men in his position who would have taken advantage of Kitty and, yes, he was ruthless in business. But he would never exploit people in that way. He knew what it felt like to be subject to the whims of another, and it was a feeling he would never willingly inflict on someone else.

He glanced past her at the mirror above the bar, his gaze focusing on their reflections, and as he watched the wariness fade from her eyes he quickly closed off his mind against the ache in his groin. It was time to change the subject.

His eyes dropped to the glass of orange juice in her hand. 'You know drinking that is practically a criminal offence in Cuba?'

She smiled. 'I wanted to end the evening with some memories, not a hangover— Sorry.' She shook her head. 'I didn't mean to sound so prim and uptight, it's just… Well, I had this idea. I thought I might find some inspiration—you know, for the rums. But I think I'm just going to end up with a sore throat from having to shout all evening.'

She glanced away and, following her gaze, he met her eyes in the mirror. For a moment they just stared at one another, and then she turned to face him. 'Look, I don't suppose you want to go somewhere a bit less rowdy...'

He felt his heart beat expectantly in his throat. Her voice was light, her expression the question mark that she had left off the end of the sentence.

Behind him the room felt solid against his back, but he could still feel the imprint of her hip on his skin, glowing red-gold like an ember.

There was no reason to say yes—every reason, in fact, to refuse. But he already knew that making her off-limits would simply exacerbate his hunger. His stomach tightened and, remembering that he hadn't actually eaten, he felt a rush of clarity. He'd make this about *that* kind of hunger.

He nodded slowly. 'Actually, I'd like that. Have you eaten?'

Her eyes were dark, almost purple, and he knew even before she shook her head that she hadn't. 'Okay... Well, I haven't either, so why don't you join me for dinner?'

'How do you like your food?'

Putting down her fork, Kitty smiled. 'It's excellent. I really love these—what are they called in Spanish again?' She gestured towards her plate.

'Boniatos,' César said softly.

She repeated it carefully, ignoring the leap in her stomach as his green eyes rested on her face. 'They're delicious. Everything is amazing.'

'I hope I didn't drag you away from your evening.'

She shook her head. 'No, not at all. I was beginning to worry that I might have to start complaining about the music being too loud—so thank you for saving me.'

She pulled herself up short. *That wasn't the image she wanted to project.*

'Not that I needed saving,' she added quickly. 'I'm not some damsel in distress.'

He stared at her impassively. 'I should be the one thanking you. You saved me from having to dine alone.'

Her heart was pounding. She still couldn't quite get her head around how the evening had unfolded. She'd met the other girls, as arranged, and walking with them through the streets she'd been struck by how different the city seemed at night. The old-school glamour was still there, but there was also something rawer—a hum of energy and excitement. Everywhere people were talking, flirting and kissing in time to the salsa spilling out of every window.

It had all looked so natural, so easy and uncomplicated, and as they'd gone into the bar she'd wondered how it would feel if she could let her body follow its desires.

Her mouth felt dry. Which, roughly translated, meant César Zayas.

And then, just like that, she'd turned around and found him standing behind her, his green eyes capturing the light like polished emeralds.

Had she imagined such a moment? Truthfully, yes. But the shock had still been electric, her response so visceral in its intensity that she'd actually forgotten to breathe.

And that was how she'd first met this man whose warm lips and urgent hands had filled her head for weeks. Breathless, self-conscious, her eyes wide with shock.

The way she'd behaved that evening had been so out

of character, and the likelihood of seeing him again so remote, she'd convinced herself that meeting him again would be a little awkward but manageable. But the moment she'd turned around she'd realised that she was nowhere near cool or sophisticated enough simply to brush off having sex with a stranger who had then turned out to be her boss.

It had been tempting simply to pretend to ignore what had happened, but she knew from past experience that it would be better to know the worst. Like whether César Zayas's idea of a 'clean slate' meant removing all reminders of what happened that evening—including her.

But of course he had been completely unfazed, and it had been his response that had prompted her invitation, to prove to herself as much as to him that the line they'd crossed seven weeks ago had been a one-off.

Clandestina, the restaurant he'd chosen, was like nowhere she'd ever been. There was no sign outside, for a start, just a doorman in a dark suit who had nodded silently, stepping back to let them pass into the Art Deco apartment block. But as they'd walked out onto the rooftop terrace she'd forgotten to breathe.

She'd been told that Cuban restaurants tended towards the rustic, but this was no homely *paladar*. It was wall-to-wall luxury. Only there weren't any walls—just a polished concrete floor, hot pink velvet-covered chairs and uninterrupted views of the city and the sea beneath a black, silk-lined awning.

She had felt almost dizzy. It was a million miles away from the shabby local pub where she and Jimmy had used to get lunch sometimes. It was pure indulgence—a sensory and sensual overload that bordered on the decadent.

She wondered if that was why he'd chosen it, or whether it was because he was friends with the owners, two brothers called Héctor and Frank. Either way, he clearly felt at home as he was on first-name terms with most of the waiters, and ordered without so much as glancing at the handwritten menu.

Or perhaps it was just the food, she thought, her stomach rumbling as the waiters brought out more plates of the most amazing pulled pork, roast chicken and *frituras de malanga*.

'So where do you see yourself professionally in the next five years? Presumably there's nothing left for you career-wise in England.'

She blinked. She had been a little nervous about the potential for lulls in their conversation, but it had been surprisingly easy and fast-flowing. They had talked mostly about work. And she'd been happy to discuss distilling and sugar cane shortages. But this aspect, her career, was not somewhere she was prepared to go. To talk about the future would risk revealing too much about her past...about Jimmy and their life together.

'I haven't thought about it.'

He frowned. 'Then you should.'

His directness knocked her off balance.

'I don't like to plan ahead.' She swallowed. 'Things don't always work out—'

He frowned, and that mask—the one without expression that he'd worn as he'd left her villa—slipped over his face.

'Dos Rios is a major step up for you. You need to build on that. Your career is international now. Or is there a reason you need to go back to England?'

After all the generic boss-new-employee questions,

his sudden trespass into more personal territory rasped against her skin.

He looked at her curiously and for one terrible moment, she thought he might press her, but after a moment, he shrugged.

It was time to change the subject, she thought. 'So how do you know them? Héctor and Frank, I mean?'

He stared at her so intently in the silence that followed her remark that the greenness of his eyes almost overwhelmed her.

'We used to hang out at the same beaches when we were teenagers,' he said finally. 'And we carried on hanging out through university, and during the holidays, until we all got jobs.'

It was not difficult to imagine the chubby, smiling brothers lolling on wooden chairs on the honey-coloured sand of some palm-strewn beach. César, on the other hand... She stared at him speculatively. He looked poised, unruffled, immaculate. He was dressed in his customary uniform of black suit and tie, although on him it seemed more like armour than clothes.

'You don't seem convinced.'

His eyes met hers and she made a face. 'Well, I can't really imagine you on a beach. Do you tuck your tie into your swim shorts?'

He smiled, and her heart skipped a beat. The table suddenly seemed to small.

'I haven't always worn a shirt and tie,' he said softly. 'I still don't when the occasion requires it.'

The memory of his naked body pressed against hers collided with a 3D image of him rising out of the sea, water trickling down his smooth golden skin. Inhaling sharply, she bit her lip—and then instantly wished she hadn't as his gaze dropped to her mouth.

'But I have to admit it was tricky getting the sand out of my laptop.'

His green eyes glittered and she bit her lip again, but her mouth defied her and she could feel herself smiling.

'Don't you have people to do that for you? I mean, you are the boss.'

The air around them felt hot and tight.

'I'm not always the boss. Sometimes I take the day or the night off.'

Her breathing was suddenly staccato, and she felt her calm mood of moments earlier flee, dissipating in the face of his untempered masculinity and authority like dandelion seeds in the wind. It was time to move the conversation away from the tempting, stealthy undercurrent beneath his words.

'So, what did you do, then, on these beaches?'

'Probably exactly what you did when you were that age.'

Kitty blinked. At 'that age' she'd been trying to fit in lectures around Jimmy's hospital appointments. There had been no time to go the beach.

'Like what?'

He shrugged. 'A whole crowd of us would hook up. You know, have some drinks, make a barbecue, play music, dance.' He raised an eyebrow. 'What?'

'Nothing.'

He shifted forward in his seat so that his knee brushed against hers beneath the table, and she had to clench her muscles to stop herself from pressing back, from leaning in to the heat of his body.

'Why are you smiling like that?'

His mood had shifted, he seemed lighter and more relaxed. It was a glimpse of a younger, less guarded man, and she wondered what had changed him over the years.

She shook her head. 'You can dance?'

'I'm Cuban—we practically invented dancing. So, yes, I can dance.'

His smile beckoned to her across the table, warm, teasing, complicit. She could feel the rise and fall of her breath, hear the sound of her heartbeat inside her head, and she had that sense of standing on the wing of a plane, of freedom and anticipation, as his eyes looked directly into hers.

'Prove it,' she said softly.

CHAPTER FIVE

THEY REACHED THE nightclub just before one. On the tenth floor of the Hotel Bello, the members-only Club el Moré was clearly *the* place to go for Havana's elite.

'You won't find any tourists here,' César said as a waiter guided them to a table.

She smiled. 'Am I not a tourist?'

He shook his head. 'You live here. That makes you an honorary *habanera.*'

A pulse sidestepped across her skin as she sat down, and she felt inexplicably happy at his choice of words. 'So is that why you come here? No tourists?'

His mouth turned up at the corners. 'Yes.'

His blunt answer made her burst out laughing. 'Really?'

He shook his head in time with the smile curving his mouth. 'No, not really. I mean, it can feel a little like you're living in a theme park—with all the cars and cigars—but really I come here because they have the best live music and cocktails in the city.'

As though reading his lips, a waiter appeared at his elbow and expertly slid two exquisite coupe glasses decorated with silver polka dots onto the table. He tapped her glass of orange juice, and then took a sip of his daiquiri.

'I don't normally drink these—' he said.

'Too touristy?' She finished his sentence.

His eyes gleamed. 'A little.'

'So what do you drink?'

'I prefer a highball of eight-year-old Dos Rios with a couple of drops of water to open it up and a little ice to push back the sweetness.' Twisting his glass around, he gazed at it assessingly. 'But tonight a daiquiri feels right—after all, one of your countrymen supposedly had a hand in its creation.'

She shook her head. Some people claimed that in an attempt to ward off scurvy Sir Francis Drake had added limes to the crew's ration of rum, but there were plenty of others who argued that the legendary cocktail had been named after a beach just off Santiago called Daiquiri.

'Anyway, *salud por que la belleza sobra*,' César said, making the usual Cuban toast. Lowering his glass, he pushed it across the table. 'Here, try it.'

He was lounging in his seat, his arm resting against the armrest, but despite his languid manner she sensed that he was watching her, waiting for her response.

Picking up his glass, Kitty took a sip. Her tastebuds exploded. It was divine.

I could get used to this, she thought, her distiller's brain sifting through the classic flavours of lime juice, sugar syrup, and of course rum. And she wasn't just talking about the alcohol, she realised a little guiltily after the first sip.

Heart pounding, she gazed slowly round the room. Both the atmosphere and the decor were completely different from the shoulder-bumping, sweaty tangle at Bar Mango.

Here, everything seemed to gleam and glitter—particularly the men and woman entwined on the velvet banquettes. The women were uniformly gorgeous and sleek. Bare-shouldered and long-limbed, their glossy lips and gleaming white teeth were almost brighter than their jewels. Sitting beside them, beneath a haze of blue-grey cigar smoke, the men looked darkly handsome in their flawless suits.

She glanced over to the dance floor. It was already crowded, and she wondered if and when he was going to respond to her challenge. Thanks to some classes at her local village hall she knew how to salsa, but somehow she didn't think that dancing with Lizzie was going to be much preparation for partnering César.

Her mouth felt suddenly dry, and with an effort she diverted her thoughts back to the drink she was holding. 'It's delicious.'

'It should be. They make it to their own unique recipe.'

She read the challenge in his eyes and tasted it again, trying to pin down the flavour. 'There's grapefruit…'

He nodded, and she felt her stomach grow warm at the approval in his green gaze. Feeling self-conscious, she took another sip, using the glass as a shield against her face.

'It tweaks it, but it's the rum that's making the magic. As it should do, Señor Zayas, given it's one of yours. The four-year-old, I believe?'

He smiled then—a smile that made a pulse beat fast in her throat.

'Bravo, Ms Quested.' Lifting his glass, he tilted it in her direction. 'For someone so young and untrained you have an impressive focus.'

He was only admiring her palate, that mystical ability to detect balance, length and complexity, but, looking up into his eyes, she felt her heart jab against her ribs like a boat bumping its moorings.

It was stupid to let herself be so affected. If she'd been his accountant, and he'd complimented her for reducing his tax bill, would she be feeling like this? Only here, in this beautiful room, with his dark eyes resting on her face, it was hard not to respond, not to bask just for a moment in the spotlight of male attention.

It had been so long. Five years, in fact. And she missed it—missed *him*: Jimmy.

He had always made her feel so special, and now she was alone. Not completely—obviously she had Lizzie and Bill and her parents. But it was a long time since she'd spent any time on her own with a man, and this man made her feel as though she was riding a roller-coaster.

But compliments couldn't change the facts, and he was still her boss. And even if he wasn't she didn't need, or want, a repeat performance.

Her cheeks felt hot.

Okay, that was a lie. She did want him. But a lone sexual encounter with a stranger to remind herself that she was still a woman was one thing... Acting on that desire *again* would be reckless and complicated and stupid.

His position as CEO of Dos Rios wasn't even the main reason why what had happened between them could only ever be a one-off. That was down to her. She didn't want intimacy or commitment, and nor did she have it in her to share such things with someone else.

Not since Jimmy. And nothing was going to change that, whatever people said about time being a great healer.

So, keeping on with all these formalities was not only unnecessary but counterproductive, for surely it implied that without them she was at risk of losing control, when in reality, without the high emotion of an accident driving them together, there was no risk at all of what had happened at her villa recurring.

It had been a one-off, she knew her own mind, and she wasn't looking to be seduced.

She cleared her throat. 'Thank you—but, please, could you call me Kitty? Being called "Ms Quested" makes me feel like I'm in a job interview.'

Her heart skittered in her chest as his gaze locked on hers. Her skin was suddenly covered with goosebumps and she felt her nipples harden.

'If that's what you'd prefer.'

She nodded, and his mouth curved upwards slowly.

'In that case, would you dance with me, Kitty?'

As they walked out onto the dance floor she felt her stomach drop as his fingers grazed against hers. He was the most beautiful man she had ever seen. Everything about him was perfect, from the long dark lashes that grazed his cheeks to those arresting green eyes.

Of course he was a beautiful dancer. Light, fluid...he didn't just follow the music, he was part of it. Like all great partners, he seemed instinctively aware of other dancers, finding a path seamlessly between the couples circling the floor, and yet she felt as though he was entirely focused on her.

And all she could think about was him. The way his eyes rested on her face, the light press of his hand gently curving around her waist. It was such a long time since she'd felt so free, so light, so young.

The band changed tempo, and as the music slowed the shifting crowd of dancers seemed to shrink around them. She felt his hand tighten against her back, the heat of his grip seeping through the fabric of her dress. Their bodies were closer now: too close. She was conscious of the solidity of his shoulder beneath her hand and he smelled so good—a kind of clean, masculine scent that made her long to lean into him.

Only she couldn't let herself do that, for if she gave in to that longing she knew where it would lead. And where it would end. But for some reason, right now, that realisation didn't seem to be carrying any weight.

Everything was snarled up inside her—desire and fear, impatience and guilt, her need to keep her distance clashing with an urge to brush her lips against his.

'I'm losing you.'

'What?'

She glanced up at him, her eyes widening with shock that he could read her so well. White and pink and yellow strobe lights above the dance floor were criss-crossing between them, dappling his skin in gold shadows, highlighting the curve of his jaw and cheeks. He looked like the profile on a coin and she had to hold back from reaching up and touching his face.

'You're tensing up. Just let it go.'

He was staring directly into her eyes, and she felt her belly clench as the rum and his nearness and her own tingling hunger began to curl around her brain. Looking at him hurt—but not so much as wanting him.

'Let it all go,' he said softly.

Her hand tightened against his shoulder and her hips

drew closer to his, their bodies blurring into one. It was as if she was floating. Everything felt soft-edged, enchanted.

Around her the room seemed to be slowing down in time to the music, and the song's chorus was chiming in time to a melting ache deep and low down. It was way past midnight. She'd been alone with him for hours. But if someone had asked her, she would have said it had been no more than minutes.

Her heart jumped. So why did she feel as if they had always known each other?

His head dropped. His face was so close that she could feel his breath coming fast and warm against her cheek. And then his eyes locked with hers, the green of them so deep and unending that it felt as though she were drowning in them.

She could fight it, could push to the surface—but she didn't want to. Blindly, she reached up and ran her fingers over the first rough trace of stubble, seeing, sensing, feeling a need that was as palpable as her own. And then, standing up on her toes, she closed her eyes and kissed him—not gently, but fiercely, forcefully, with a hunger she had never felt for any man but him.

As their mouths touched he pulled her towards him, parting her lips with his, splaying his warm hands across her back.

She moaned softly. Her breasts were aching and she could feel every contour of his hard, muscular body. Only she wanted more. Wanted the touch of his hands sliding over her skin and the frenzied release that she knew they would bring.

She had missed him.

Pleasure danced across her skin. The blood was racing along her limbs as though towards some imaginary finishing line.

And then suddenly something shifted inside her. This intimacy was too much. Her pulse was beating too hard and too fast.

Her heart punching against her ribs, she pulled away. Silencing the tingling heat that was creeping over her skin, she opened her eyes and the room jolted back into focus.

The lights were too bright. She wanted to close her eyes. And her body was humming, the imprints of his hands stinging fiercely on her skin.

'Excuse me—'

She felt dazed, unsteady—and, not wanting to meet his gaze, she spun round and walked swiftly off the dance floor, her legs moving automatically like some wind-up toy.

'Kitty—'

They had reached the table and she turned reluctantly to face him. He was standing beside her, his hand resting on the back of a chair, and she tried her best to rebuild the barriers she had so casually smashed with one careless kiss.

'I'm sorry,' she said. 'I shouldn't have done that.'

He frowned. '"Shouldn't" usually implies a level of duty or obligation to something. Or someone.'

His voice was quiet, but there was a tension there that hadn't been there before—one that matched the set of his jaw.

'I thought you were a free agent.'

He let the words hang in the air between them.

Her throat tightened. 'I am. That wasn't what I meant.'

She clenched her hands. She was making a total mess of what she was trying to say, but she had so little experience of this kind of conversation.

He took a step forward, his green eyes searching her face. 'You look pale. Here, sit down.'

She shook her head. 'It's so hot in here. I think I need some fresh air.'

But it was more than that. She could sense it…just out of reach, in the corner of her mind…like the answer to a crossword clue or a forgotten name that went with a face.

He led her out of the nightclub into the foyer. The cool air restored her a little, but her legs still felt as though they weren't connected to her body.

Incredibly, the ladies' cloakroom was empty.

On another night, perhaps if she'd still been out with Carrie and the other girls, she might have taken a photo and sent it to Lizzie, for the ladies' room was gloriously over the top, with gilt-edged mirrors and a chandelier hanging from the ceiling. But right now she felt too on edge to enjoy the flamboyant decor.

Turning on the tap, she held her wrists under the cooling water and stared at her reflection in the mirror. César was right. Her face did look pale, and her eyes were wide and feverish.

Except she didn't feel ill. Just not herself.

You're just tired, she told her reflection. *You've been working too hard, and it was a shock meeting him like this tonight.*

Her cheeks felt suddenly warm again. And, of course, she'd kissed him. *Again.*

What was happening to her?

She'd hoped that Cuba would bring a change to her

life, but when she was with César she just didn't recognise herself. Gone was the sensible, shy, small-town girl and in her place was a wild, passionate woman who acted without thinking.

But it had to stop here.

It didn't matter that he looked like an angel, or that his touch turned her inside out with ecstasy. In fact, that was a reason *not* to give in to her desire. She didn't want to want this dazzling, uncompromising man who threatened to bring passion and emotion into her world. For emotions were as dangerous and random as life itself, twisting and transforming, so that love turned to loss and passion to pain in a heartbeat.

And she was an adult. She could feel attracted to him and not act on it.

Breathing out slowly, she opened her handbag and found her compact. She tilted her face upwards and dusted some blusher across her cheeks. That was better. Now it just needed some lipstick. Where was it?

Frowning, she felt inside her bag, and then tipped the contents out onto the counter.

There it was.

Picking up the tube, she swiped it carefully across her lips, blotted them with a tissue and then swiped again. That would have to do.

She dropped the lipstick back into her bag and began to pick up the other items, and as she did so her hand froze. Gazing down at the box of tampons, she felt her stomach flip over, and then a rush of panic, cold and dark and swift-moving like floodwater, swept over her skin.

Gripping the side of the counter, she steadied her legs.

She couldn't be.

Probably she had her dates wrong.

With an effort, she worked her way back through the calendar. But there was no doubt. She was at least five weeks late.

Tilting his wrist, César glanced down at his watch and frowned. He didn't usually stand around waiting for women to come out of cloakrooms, and Kitty seemed to be taking an unusually long time, but he felt responsible for her.

The thought jarred. Feeling responsible, feeling anything aside from desire was not something he'd anticipated, but he knew that he had no choice. Right now she was his responsibility.

He wondered again why she was taking so long. Remembering her flushed cheeks, he grimaced. She was obviously embarrassed—or had he been too vehement when she'd pulled away? His chest tightened. Maybe...

But he was only human, and *she* had kissed *him*, leaning into his body so that he'd been able to feel her heart vibrating, her fingers caressing his face. And everything had faded. The lights, the music, the tension in his body—everything had turned to dust, spinning into the darkness. Everything except Kitty.

He thought back to how she'd melted into him, the heat and the hunger of her kiss and the softness of her mouth. His breath caught in his throat. She had made his head spin, made his body ache. And he'd wanted more. Only as suddenly as she'd started it she had pulled away. So, yes, he had been a little terse.

He gritted his teeth. He should never have asked her to dinner. In fact he should never have come back to

Cuba. If he'd just kept to his schedule he would be in the Bahamas, asleep, serene and oblivious.

Instead his body felt as if it was about to fly apart.

Suddenly he saw her, and his heart started to pound. There was colour on her cheeks, still, but she didn't look embarrassed—more stunned.

'Is everything okay?'

She nodded stiffly. 'Yes, it's fine. Thank you.' Her eyes didn't meet his. 'I'm a little out of practice when it comes to going out on the town.'

'Of course.' In other words, she wanted to go home. He felt a momentary pang of regret that the evening was ending, but then pulled out his phone. 'I'll call my driver.'

The drive home to the estate took less than twenty minutes. Usually he liked the clear night-time roads, but tonight he felt a little conflicted, for a part of him wanted to delay the moment when he and Kitty returned to being Señor Zayas and Ms Quested.

Glancing over to where Kitty sat beside him, her eyes fixed on the window, he felt his muscles tighten. Although perhaps that moment had already happened.

Her villa was in sight now. Feeling the car slow, he leaned forward and tapped on the glass behind Rodolfo's head. 'You can drop me with Ms Quested. I need to stretch my legs,' he said in Spanish. 'So I'll make my own way up to the house.'

As the car drove away Kitty gazed up at him warily.

It was not dark. A beautiful pearlescent moon spread a clear white light over the villa. But he'd been raised to walk women to their front doors.

'I'll walk you in.'

'Thank you,' she said quietly.

Inside, the villa was dark, but she switched on a table lamp and instantly a warm yellow glow spread across the room. He waited for her to say goodnight. Waited for her to smile politely and thank him for a wonderful evening. But she didn't speak.

He stared at her tense, set face, trying to interpret her silence. And then he shut the door quietly. 'Look, I'm sorry about what I said at the club.'

He stared past her across the living room and then instantly wished he hadn't as he caught sight of the sofa. His body hardened painfully as an image of the pair of them, half-naked and panting, played inside his head.

With an effort, he forced his mind away from the memory and dragged his gaze back to her face. 'I was out of order.'

'Actually, I kissed *you*, so if anyone was out of order it was me.'

He thought back to the disturbed nights and restless days he'd endured since walking out of this villa. He might have left her in Cuba, but she had never left his thoughts, and had he not been her boss he would have kissed her first in the club.

'It doesn't matter,' he said truthfully. 'We crossed that line seven weeks ago. Left it for dust on that couch.'

'That doesn't make it right.'

Watching her face stiffen, he felt a rush of frustration. A planned life was a life free of complication, because there were rules and boundaries. This kind of twisting, awkward conversation was exactly why he didn't leave his libido in charge of his actions.

Worse, in this room, with the ghost of their passionate encounter still tangible, her remoteness was setting his teeth on edge. Between leaving the dance floor and coming out of the cloakroom something had changed. But what?

He stared down at her uncertainly, reluctant to know more but even more reluctant to turn away. 'Has something happened?'

A quick breath lifted her shoulders. 'I don't know. It might have. Or it might not. I'm not sure—' She broke off mid-sentence.

Beneath his shirt, his heart started to pound. Her words made no sense, but it was her sudden retreat into silence that made the tension in his chest suddenly unbearable. For he had learned from Celia that the unsayable was always worse than anything that could be spoken out loud, no matter how inarticulately expressed.

Gazing down at her pale, set face, he felt his muscles tighten, and suddenly he knew why she couldn't speak. 'I'm sure you'll be fine,' he said coolly. 'But if you're that worried why don't you call your boyfriend?'

He felt a sharp sting of anger just saying the word, but he was grateful to have found out the truth now rather than later.

She was shaking her head. 'I don't have a boyfriend. I told you that—'

'I know what you told me, but that doesn't make it true.'

'I'm not lying to you.' Her eyes were narrowing and a flush of colour was slipping slowly over the contours of her face. 'I'm trying to tell you the truth.'

'It's a little too late for that.'

He knew his anger was disproportionate. They'd had

sex only once, but it was disconcerting to discover that he still had this weakness inside, this impaired judgement.

Her mouth twisted. 'Not really. I only realised tonight.'

'Realised what?'

She hesitated, and his anger flared hotter.

'I'm not about to start playing guessing games, Kitty.'

'I didn't—' She licked her lips. 'I think I might be pregnant.'

Whatever he'd been expecting her to say, it hadn't been that. He stared at her in silence, brain reeling, body rigid with shock. 'How do you—?'

'How do I know?' She bit her lip. 'I don't—for sure. But I'm five weeks late.'

He did the maths inside his head. It worked. Only...

'I thought you said you couldn't have children?'

The accusatory tone and the implied doubt in his words seemed magnified in the small room. He watched her face close over.

'I didn't think I could.' She looked up at him, her eyes too bright, and he could almost see her retreating. 'I'm sorry. I shouldn't have told you.'

His stomach twisted. She looked drained, and young, too young to be dealing with this alone in a foreign country, away from her family. Having wrongly accused her of lying, he could hardly condemn her for honesty.

'No, I'm glad you told me.'

And, despite his shock, he was surprised to find that he actually was. The truth was always preferable to being fed lies. But this was too big a truth to tackle now. Out of habit, he schooled his features into a mask of calm, the CEO in him taking charge.

'Look, it's late. We can't do anything more tonight and you look exhausted.' He glanced across the room. 'You need to go to bed.'

She shook her head. 'I don't think I can sleep.'

'Then just lie down for a minute.'

Gently, he guided her towards the sofa. He watched her sit down. She seemed hardly aware of him, and he realised that she was as exhausted as she looked.

'Come on.' He grabbed a cushion. 'Put your head on this and just close your eyes.'

She slid off her shoes and lay down, curling onto her side, looking up at him with half-lidded eyes.

'We'll talk about this in the—' he began, but she was already asleep, her hair spreading out like a fan of flames over her shoulders. Shrugging his jacket from his shoulders, he draped it carefully over her body.

Dropping down onto one of the chairs, he shifted against the cushions, trying to get comfortable. He thought back to how this evening had started. Seeing Kitty through the car window, following her into the bar, dancing with her...and then that kiss.

It had been the most tantalising foreplay in what he'd hoped would be a night as passionate as that first time. What he hadn't expected was to find out that he might be a father.

His chest tightened. Mixing a night of incredible sex with a complete loss of control had been a cocktail to rival any daiquiri, only now it appeared that there might be life-changing consequences to that explosive encounter on her sofa.

He felt shattered, his head spinning with a dizzying

rush of unanswered questions, but the answers would have to wait until morning.

Tilting his head back, he took one last look at the woman who was going to give him those answers and then closed his eyes.

CHAPTER SIX

SOMEWHERE, SOMEONE WAS singing about her heart being broken.

Shifting onto her side, Kitty lay with her eyes closed, still half asleep, but following the words. It was a song that was playing everywhere in Havana—only why was it playing inside her villa?

Slowly she opened her eyes and sat up.

There was no sign of César but, glancing down, she realised she hadn't been sleeping under a blanket but his jacket, and the chair opposite the sofa had been moved. Her heart gave a leap as she noticed the indentation in the cushion.

He must have stayed the night— only surely men like César Zayas didn't kip on chairs in people's living rooms.

And then she smelled the coffee.

Standing up, she walked into the kitchen. Her coffee pot sat on the counter. She didn't need to touch it to know it was hot. Steam was still drifting out of the spout.

And there on the back doorstep, a cup in his hand, was César.

She almost turned and ran. Last night she might have been brave or stupid enough to share her fears, but this morning she simply wasn't up to facing him. Particularly as she had turned his world upside down over what must surely be a mistake.

She *couldn't* be pregnant.

Last night had been the emotional equivalent of a ride at the funfair. Bumping into him like that, that kiss on the dance floor… She hadn't been thinking straight, and in the cloakroom she'd panicked and put two and two together and come up with a pregnancy. Surely though, there was some other, less dramatic reason for her symptoms. One that she could best identify on her own, in private.

But before she had a chance to move he turned, and her legs unhelpfully stopped working. For a moment he stared at her in silence, and then he straightened up. He was standing on the bottom step, so that his brilliant green eyes were level with hers, and it took every shred of willpower not to look away.

Even though the clean lines of his face were slightly smudged by sleep, the shock of his beauty made her head spin. Her heart was beating so hard that she could feel her ribs vibrating. She knew she had to say something, but her brain seemed to have shut down in sympathy with her legs.

'How do you feel?' he said quietly.

His gaze drifted down over her body and then slowly back up to her face, and she remembered that she was still wearing her clothes from the night before.

But then so was he.

He'd lost the tie, but he was still wearing his shirt and suit trousers, and the crumpled state of the shirt together with the stubble darkening his jawline was the final piece of evidence confirming what she already knew.

'I'm okay. So, you stayed the night?' She paused. 'Did you sleep in the chair?'

He nodded. 'It was fine.' He held up his cup. 'I hope you don't mind—I made myself a coffee.'

She shook her head. 'No, of course not.'

It felt strange. Not awkward, just astonishing that this man might be connected to her by more than that brief but blinding solar flare of passion.

'Would you like a cup?'

She shook her head again. 'No, thank you. I don't really like the taste at the moment.'

A breeze stirred the air between them, loosening her hair, and she tucked it behind her ear, grateful for something to do as his eyes rested on her face.

'We need to talk,' he said finally. 'Shall we go inside?'

She nodded.

He followed her into the kitchen. 'First things first, you need to take a test.' He met her eyes, blank-faced.

She stared at him dazedly. Everything was moving so fast. Her brain kept jumping back and forth—to the past, to England and Jimmy, then back to the present. Too fast.

In all honesty, she wasn't absolutely ready to know the truth yet—but then she could hardly drop a grenade in his lap, as she had last night, and expect him to sit there and hold the pin indefinitely.

'Yes, I do.' She frowned. 'Do I need to go to a doctor? Or can I get one at a pharmacy?'

'You don't have to worry about that. Here.' He reached past her and picked up a nondescript brown envelope from the counter.

'I had one of my people get a test for you. Don't

worry, he's very discreet. He understands this is a personal matter.'

She nodded mutely, unsure whether she was more shocked by the cool-headed speed and efficiency of his behaviour or the fact that this man might be the father of her unborn child.

Her hand trembled slightly as she took the envelope. Despite his dishevelled appearance—or probably because of it—he looked incredibly sexy. Even rumpled, the formality of his clothes seemed to accentuate the raw masculinity of the body beneath, and his hair looked as it had after they'd made love. Although it was obviously him and not her who had run hands through it one too many times on this occasion—and not in passion but through worry.

For a moment she thought he was going to say something, or that she should. It seemed as if something should be said, but what was the correct choice of words for this situation?

'I'll use the bathroom,' she said unnecessarily.

Closing the bathroom door, she breathed out raggedly. Her hands were shaking a lot now, and she tore at the box clumsily. The instructions were written in English—not that she needed them. She'd taken dozens of tests when she'd tried to get pregnant before, but she still read them through carefully, just to make sure. She'd been careless enough already.

There—it was done.

She gazed down at the stick. It seemed unreasonable that such a small disposable object should carry such heavy expectations: hope and despair, excitement and disappointment, all wrapped up in a tiny piece of plastic.

Her heart was beating erratically, and suddenly she badly wanted to ring Lizzie—only her phone was in her bag, and her bag was wherever she'd left it last night.

But even as she reached for the door handle she knew this wasn't something she could share with anyone but the man who was waiting patiently in her kitchen...

He was standing where she'd left him.

'We have to wait now,' she said quickly, putting the stick down on the counter. 'For three minutes.'

His face was impassive. But then he didn't love her, and this hypothetical baby wasn't planned. It didn't stop her wondering, though, how he would have looked if the situation was different? Would he have held her hand as they waited? Or discreetly checked his watch to check the time.

Her throat tightened. And when it was negative would he have pulled her into his arms and told her that it didn't matter? That next time would be different.

'Why did you become a distiller?'

She glanced up at him, startled. Why was he asking her that now?

'I have a chemistry degree.'

'The two aren't necessarily connected,' he said gently.

She stared at him in silence. She'd been planning to do a Masters in polymers after graduating, but then Jimmy had been diagnosed with cancer and it had been a struggle even to finish her degree.

Naturally everyone had wanted to help, and she had been happy...no, *grateful*...to take a step back, to let other people—doctors and nurses, her friends and of course her family—make the decisions and take charge of the situation. They had helped her care for Jimmy, and then to grieve for him.

But after time she'd realised that somewhere along the line she had taken one step back too many. She had never been an extrovert like Lizzie—never been bold or loud. But after Jimmy's death she'd felt diminished, defeated, and so very tired of life. No amount of coaxing and cajoling could persuade her to leave the house.

And then Bill had asked her to help him at the distillery. Lizzie had set it up, of course, guessing correctly that she would always put other people's needs above her own.

Remembering that first winter when she'd started working for Blackstrap, she almost smiled. The former salt shed was made of stone, and the distillery had been freezing. But she hadn't cared. She had been too busy playing with spices, pulling on the knowledge acquired from her degree, blending and tweaking and chasing that elusive perfect flavour.

And working on the rum hadn't just woken her taste buds, it had woken her from a kind of self-imposed hibernation. It had reminded her that she was still alive, and that even if she was alone she needed to live that life. Only now there might be a new life growing inside of her.

'My brother-in-law asked me to help him. It was Bill's idea to set up Blackstrap, but he was having a few problems with the flavour profile. He's got the technical know-how, but he's not very good at focusing.'

'Luckily for him, you are.'

She stared at him in confusion. Why were they talking about her sister's boyfriend? Surely he wasn't interested in Bill and his lack of focus.

And then, as he glanced casually at his watch, she knew why. He had been trying to distract her.

'I think it's probably been three minutes,' he said quietly.

Her heart contracted. Suddenly she couldn't breathe.

'It's okay.' Reaching out, he took her hand and squeezed it. 'Do you want me to look first?'

'No.' She shook her head and picked up the stick.

Her throat tightened and suddenly it was hard to balance on her feet without gripping the counter. For a dizzying second she pictured Jimmy's face, his smile, his tears.

Pregnant 3+

She looked up at César. 'It's positive.'

His expression didn't change by so much as a tremor.

'I'm pregnant.'

She knew that these tests were ninety-nine per cent accurate, but somehow saying the words out loud made it feel more real. It was there—in her hand. She was going to have a baby.

Only the person who was supposed to be the father, supposed to be there with her, was no longer around.

Her heartbeat had slowed; she felt as if she was in a dream. 'I'm pregnant,' she said again.

César's grip tightened around her hand, and as she met his gaze she felt her legs wilt. His eyes were so very green, and for a moment all she could think was that they should be brown.

Her head was swimming. It had taken five years, but most days she was content with her life. She still regretted Jimmy's death, but the acute pain, that hollowed-out ache of despair, had faded a few years ago. Only now this news had reawakened old emotions.

He caught her arm. 'You need to sit down.'

Still holding her hand, he led her into the living room. She sat down on the sofa. The first shock was starting to wear off and panic was starting to ripple over her skin.

'I don't understand how this could happen.'

When she and Jimmy had started trying for a baby he had been so keen he'd taken a fertility test and every-thing had been normal. She'd been about to get herself checked out when he fell ill, and then there had been too much going on, other more urgent tests to take and so each time she wasn't pregnant she had blamed her-self—her periods had always been irregular. Only now it seemed as though it hadn't been her.

César sat down beside her. 'I'm pretty sure it hap-pened the usual way.'

She stared at him dazedly. Her head was a muddle of emotions, but he was so calm. So reasonable.

'You haven't asked me,' she said slowly, 'if the baby could be someone else's.'

In a way, that was more of a shock than her preg-nancy. With hindsight—her late period, her sudden craving for fruit juice, her heightened relentless fa-tigue—all pointed to one obvious explanation, but she knew it was a question most men in his situation would have asked.

He leaned back a little, studying her face. There was an expression in his eyes that she couldn't fathom.

For a moment he didn't reply, and then he shrugged. 'What happened between us isn't something I've found easy to forget. I'd like to believe that you feel the same way. But if you think there's any question over my paternity now would be a good time to say so.'

She shook her head. 'There hasn't been anyone but you.' Her eyes flicked to his face. 'And, yes, I feel the same way.'

As she spoke some of the tension in her shoulders lifted. They hadn't planned for this to happen, to bring new life into the world, and they might not love one another, but those few heated moments had been fierce and important for both of them, and she was glad that this child had been conceived out of such extraordinary mutual passion.

'I don't regret it,' she said abruptly. 'What we did or what's happened.'

Her heart swelled. She had wanted and waited for this baby for so long, and suddenly all those other tests, with their accusatory ghostly white rectangles, seemed to grow vague and unsubstantial.

'Well, it's a little late for regrets.' He paused. 'This baby isn't going anywhere. What matters now is what happens next.'

What happens next?

The options revolved inside her head.

She could go home—and of course a part of her obviously desperately wanted to jump on the next plane to England. But even if César agreed to help support her financially she was going to need a job at some point.

The fog inside her brain was making it difficult to think straight.

'I suppose I should probably get an appointment with a doctor,' she said hesitantly.

He nodded. 'I can help you with that. And I *want* to help.'

He was still holding her hand. His skin was rougher than she remembered, but his voice was soft, gentle in a way that made her throat constrict.

'Thank you,' she said.

His words replayed inside her head. She imagined that a lot of men—particularly wealthy, powerful men, who liked being in control of every tiny detail of their lives—would have got extremely bent out of shape, being confronted by the unplanned pregnancy of a woman they barely knew. But César seemed remarkably unfazed.

Of course, you didn't take charge of a small-time family business and turn it into a global brand before the age of thirty unless you could handle what life threw at you. Even so, finding out you were going to be a parent was a personal and extraordinary milestone for anybody...

'You're being very kind,' she said quietly. 'Very fair.'

His gaze rested on her face. 'What happened wasn't just down to you, Kitty. We both got swept away.'

For a second they stared at one another, wide-eyed, the sound of their breathing punctuating the silence of the room as they remembered.

As Kitty stared at him she felt her heart oscillating against her ribs. The heat of his body, the swell of his muscles beneath his shirt was crowding her mind. He was so solid and male and real, and everything inside her was reaching out to him—only should she be feeling like this? Was it normal or right to feel such a strong physical need for a stranger when her heart was aching for the husband who had missed out on realising his dreams?

'Yes, we did,' she whispered.

'And now we both have to work this out. And we *can* work it out. We can work it out together.'

His eyes were boring into hers. 'If that's what you want.'

She stared at him, mesmerised by the faint trace of stubble on his jaw and the determination in his green gaze. She knew that Lizzie and Bill, and her parents, would be falling over themselves to help her, but she knew César would make this work. She trusted him to do it because managing complex, challenging situations was what he did every day, and it would be wonderful to have his support—not just for her, but for their child.

'I'd like that.'

'Good.' He smiled, and then pulled out his phone. 'I'll call the doctor first, and then I have a couple of contacts who can probably pull some strings...speed up the paperwork.'

Paperwork?

The word scraped against her skin. Presumably he was talking about some kind of financial settlement or an agreement over visiting rights, but—

'Isn't that a little premature?' She gave him a small stiff smile. 'I mean, the baby's not due for seven or eight months.'

He frowned. 'I know—and that's why you need to stop worrying about all this right now. Just concentrate on yourself and our baby, and let me deal with the wedding arrangements.'

Her ears were buzzing.

Wedding? What wedding?

She stared at him in confusion. 'I don't understand...'

His eyes dropped to her face. 'What's there to understand? You said you wanted to make this work.'

He was speaking patiently, but she could feel the tautness in his body vibrating from his fingers into hers. She felt her pulse accelerate. She hardly knew César, and she certainly didn't move in his kind of circles, but she knew enough about the world—his world—to know that making this situation 'work' didn't typically include a marriage proposal.

'I know I did,' she protested, 'and I do. But—'

'But what?'

Gone was the softness in the voice. Now he sounded as she imagined he did in the boardroom, when confronted by bad sales figures. Cool. Distant. Hostile.

'Marriage is the quickest and most efficient way to tie up all the loose ends.'

Loose ends. Was that what she and the baby were?

'I just assumed that you…' She hesitated. 'Well, that you were talking about being involved in the baby's life—not mine.'

Surely he didn't actually mean what he was saying. It must be the knee-jerk reaction of a powerful man who wanted to call the shots.

His eyes locked on hers and instantly she felt the hairs on the back of her neck stand to attention.

'Then you assumed wrong.' He shook his head. '*"Involved"?*' Frowning, he turned the word over in his mouth as though it tasted bad. 'Clearly you've already given this some thought—so tell me, Kitty. What does "involved" actually look like?' he said softly.

Kitty blinked. His hand was still holding hers and, slipping her fingers free of his, she folded her arms protectively in front of her stomach. 'I don't know, exactly, but you travel a lot for work, so I suppose you could come and visit whenever you're in London.'

His green eyes fixed on her face. 'Is that your way of telling me you're leaving Havana?'

Her breath caught in her throat and her heart stopped beating—and then began pounding like a drumroll.

'I'm not leaving Havana. Not yet, anyway.' She frowned. 'Just because I'm pregnant it doesn't mean I want to stop working.'

'But you are planning on returning to England?'

Trying to still the jittery feeling in her chest, she glanced past him at the view through the open back door. It looked so idyllic and peaceful, and it would be amazing to raise a child here in the sunshine, but Havana wasn't her home.

'Yes, of course.'

He was staring at her as if she had taken leave of her senses. 'So how exactly am I supposed to be "involved" in my child's life on that basis?'

A mix of anger and apprehension was creeping over her skin. A moment ago she had liked him, trusted him, thought that she understood him and that he understood her. How could she have got him so wrong?

But what did she really know about this man sitting beside her on the sofa?

She glared at him. 'How could you be involved in our child's life anyway? Last time you walked out of that door you told me that you didn't spend much time in Havana. And you don't. Seven weeks ago you disappeared off the face of the earth—'

'So that gives you licence to disappear off the face of the earth with my child?'

'Of course not,' she said hoarsely 'I'm just saying that I didn't know where you were or when you were coming back.'

'We had sex *once*. Of course you didn't know where I was or when I was coming back.'

The bluntness of his words brought her to her senses. Why was she even having this conversation with him? It was crazy. But he was crazier if he thought she would suddenly agree to marry him.

'I know that.' Taking a breath, she got her voice under control. 'And now I know how you feel about the baby, obviously I would love you to be involved on some level.'

He was staring at her coolly.

'On some level.' He shook his head. 'That's very gracious of you, Kitty. Would you like cash or are you happy with a bank transfer?'

She shook her head 'I don't just mean financially.' With an effort, she tried to blank out the rapid fire of her heartbeat so that she could think. 'Look, I'm not trying to sideline you. I'm just trying to deal with what's real and what's not.'

His jaw tightened. 'Then let me help you. What's real is that we had sex on this couch. Unprotected sex. Now you're pregnant with my baby, and I intend to watch him or her grow up. Not make do with a couple of snatched weekends a year when I'm passing through Europe.' He stared at her steadily. 'I grew up in a loving, family home with two parents. I want that for my child.'

Her heart felt as though it was breaking. She had wanted that too. But marrying César was not going to make that happen.

'I want that too,' she said slowly. 'But that's not an option here.'

'It is if you marry me.' His eyes were as impassive as his voice.

She breathed in sharply. Her head was swimming. She could still remember Jimmy's proposal, the tremble in his hand as he'd taken hers. He'd loved her, and he'd wanted to share his life with her. And he had, and it had been wonderful, and painful and beautiful, and she wasn't going to sully the memory of her marriage with some convenient but hollow pretence.

She shook her head slowly. 'I'm not going to marry you, César. That isn't going to change and I don't want to talk about it anymore.'

'That's not how this works.'

In reply, she stood up and walked stiffly across the room. He stared after her, and his expression of disbelief would have made her laugh—only she didn't feel like laughing.

'*Seriously?*'

'Yes, I'm serious. I don't want to talk about this anymore.'

'This is ridiculous.' His eyes were narrowed and opaque, like uncut emeralds. 'It's pointless to make things more complicated than they are. You chose to be with me.'

'No, I chose to have sex with you,' she said shakily. 'And, yes, it was amazing. But it doesn't matter how good it was. Sex is not why you get married. And neither is pregnancy. Marriage is about love and loyalty, and I am not going to stand up in front of witnesses and make vows that I don't believe. Because you shouldn't say them if you don't believe them. And we don't. I don't— I can't—'

Her voice snapped and she lowered her face, not wanting him to see the pain she was feeling, or the tears that were so close to falling.

There was a short, stunned silence, and then he took a step towards her. 'Kitty, I'm—'

She held up her hand to stop him. 'Please don't. Please. Can you just go now? Just go!'

There was another short silence, and for a moment she thought he was going to ignore her wishes, but then seconds later she heard the door shut with a click.

Looking up, she felt a sharp stab of relief and regret as she realised that the room was empty.

She was alone.

Breathing out unsteadily, César stared down at his laptop and then abruptly slammed it shut. What was the point? He'd been looking at that document for an hour now, and he hadn't read one word of it.

He gritted his teeth. Had it really just been an hour since he'd left Kitty's villa—or, to be more accurate, since she'd dismissed him? It felt like a lifetime.

After closing the door he'd walked back to the house and taken refuge in his study. There, surrounded by the familiar armour of his working life, he'd assumed that he would be able to block out those last few moments when her voice had started to shake and she'd looked close to tears.

He'd been wrong.

His stomach clenched. It had been a long time since he'd made a woman cry. In fact he knew the date exactly.

Remembering his mother's tears when he'd been forced to confess his stupidity, he felt a hot rush of shame—just as he had that day nearly ten years ago. And now he had made Kitty cry.

He swore softly. He'd handled it so badly. He'd been relentless and insensitive. Pushing his agenda as ruthlessly as he would do in business. But what did being ruthless in business matter if he was a coward in private?

He stood up abruptly, needing to move, wanting to distance himself physically from the truth. But of course there was no escaping what was inside his head.

Celia had played him. Aged twenty-four, he had been emotionally open, happy-go-lucky and painfully gullible. She had lied—not just behind his back but to his face, repeatedly—and he'd believed every word that had come out of her beautiful lying mouth. Because it had been the same beautiful mouth that had kissed him and told him she loved him.

He'd fallen for her, and in so doing he had embarrassed himself, and his parents. And he'd vowed never to let any woman have that power over him again.

Only it crushed him to live like that. To *have* to live like that. And it was a necessity. He could tell himself that it was just common sense or cool, hard logic for a man in his position to keep things flexible. That women were just pieces on the chessboard of his life. But the truth that only he knew and could acknowledge was that it was fear that kept them at arm's length. Fear of the weakness within him—that flaw in his nature that left him vulnerable to exploitation if he allowed himself to care, to feel.

Only he *did* feel something for Kitty. Desire, obviously, but also something protective that—incredibly—had nothing to do with the pregnancy.

He'd felt it out on that road when she'd looked at him, her grey eyes shining with anxiety and anger, and then again in the villa this morning, when she'd looked so stunned, so torn—

It had scared him, feeling like that, feeling anything,

and he'd been angry and frustrated with himself. So it had been easy to latch on to that frustration and turn it towards her. Not for being pregnant, but for being a soft-mouthed, smoky-eyed reminder of the mistake he'd made all those years ago and was trying so hard not to make again.

Kitty had brought chaos and passion and emotion into his world, and marriage was the logical way to restore order, and not just for himself. He knew how much his parents longed to see him married, and if he could marry and give them a grandchild he might finally atone for the pain and distress he'd caused them.

Only Kitty had other ideas. Hearing her talk had made him feel like an outsider—playing a bit part rather than being the central protagonist he so clearly was— but the harder he'd pushed the more she'd resisted.

There was a knock on the door and his heart twitched with anticipation. But almost immediately his pulse slowed as a middle-aged woman with calm brown eyes appeared in the doorway: his housekeeper, Rosa.

'Would you like some coffee, Señor Zayas?'

His chest tightened. Coffee. A conference call, and then some emails. In other words, business as usual. Except that it wasn't: everything had changed, forever.

He shook his head. 'No, thank you, Rosa. I have something I need to sort out.'

Ten minutes later he was standing in front of the door to Kitty's villa.

The garden was well kept, and the paint on the window frames shone in the sunlight. It seemed astonishing that it should look so untouched by what had happened. Surely, given the storm of revelation and confrontation that had passed through the villa that morning, there should be some sign or evidence of that turmoil, but it all looked so serene.

He tapped on the door and waited. After five minutes he tapped again, this time more loudly, but still there was no reply.

Could she have gone out? His heart began to pound, worst-case scenarios flooding his head and spilling over in panicky surges. Had he driven her out of Havana? Out of Cuba?

Pulse accelerating, he turned and walked swiftly away, circling the house towards the back door, his hand reaching for his phone. If he had to, he would send someone to the airport to stop her.

His fingers tightened around the phone—and then his legs started to slow.

On the back porch Kitty was standing with her back to him, watering some flowers. Her hair was loose and damp, probably from a shower, and she was wearing a simple slip dress. Briefly he allowed his eyes to roam over the long, slim legs and the viola-shaped back, and then, stepping forward, he cleared his throat.

She turned, her eyes widening, her expression changing from soft to guarded in a heartbeat, and his own heart began beating fast as she lowered the watering can in front of her body like a shield.

He held up his hands. 'I'm not here to fight.'

She stared at him steadily. 'So why are you here, César?'

She looked calmer, but there was a redness around her eyes and her already pale skin seemed almost translucent.

'I wanted to apologise for before.' He paused. 'I truly didn't mean to upset you. I'm just trying to do the right thing. I want to do the right thing.'

'And marrying someone you don't love is "the right thing"?'

He winced. 'When you put it like that, no, I suppose it isn't. But people marry for lots of different reasons, Kitty, in lots of different cultures. And sometimes they grow into loving one another.'

'And you think that could happen? To us?'

He was about to say yes, but there was a nakedness in her eyes that made it impossible for him to lie. 'I don't know,' he said truthfully. 'I've never been married so I couldn't say for certain. But you haven't been married either, so you can't say that it wouldn't happen.'

There was a silence. Behind her, a few petals drifted through the air like confetti.

'Actually, I have been married,' she said quietly. Her shoulders were braced but her mouth was trembling.

He stared at her, his breath suddenly leaden in his chest. 'Are you divorced?'

'Widowed.'

She looked exactly as she had done after the accident, her face taut with that same mix of strength and fragility that made him want to reach out and pull her against him.

'I'm so sorry. I had no idea.'

She nodded stiffly and, watching her fight for control, he felt an ache inside his chest.

'What was his name?'

'Jimmy.' Her face softened. 'We weren't married for very long. Only a year before he died. But we knew each other our whole lives.' She blinked. '*His* whole life anyway.'

'How long ago did it happen?' he said softly.

'Five years.'

Her answer shocked him more than finding out that she'd been married and widowed. She'd been so young to have her world implode like that.

'It isn't in your file.'

She frowned. 'No, it's not. Because I don't want it to be. It's not a secret—it's just that I don't want it to be how I'm defined.'

He could hear the tangle of emotions in her voice—the pain, the anger, the defiance.

'Do you know what I mean? Have you ever had something happen to you that you don't want to share with strangers? That's private to you?'

Her eyes were fixed on his face and he felt her question resonate through him. Thinking back to his own past, and how desperately he had tried to distance himself from his weakness and stupidity, he nodded. 'You don't have to explain yourself to me Kitty.'

'I know I don't, but I want to.' She took a step forward. 'It's not that I don't believe in love, it's that I can't believe in it. I can't feel that way again. But I don't want to pretend either.'

It took him two strides to reach her. Pulling her into his arms, he breathed out unsteadily, and then, before he even knew that it was what he wanted to do, he was lowering his face, brushing his lips over her hair and inhaling her scent.

'It's okay. I understand,' he murmured.

He felt her body tense, and then she leaned into him. Blocking off the thoughts swirling inside his mind, he rested his head against hers.

'I don't know what to do.' She looked up into his eyes. 'I don't want to be unfair. This is your child too.'

He swallowed. With her face so close to his, and

her warm, soft skin beneath his hands, everything felt possible. No obstacle was too big. Not even her past.

Or his.

'I know. And, however ineptly I expressed it before,' he replied, 'I meant what I said. I want to give my child the kind of loving family home I had. I know we can't do that as husband and wife, but is there any way we could try and find some kind of middle ground?'

'Like what?'

She was trying to be fair, but he knew that one wrong word would cause her to bolt.

'We hardly know each other, and that's only going to make everything harder in the future, when we need to be able to communicate. If you mean what you say about not being unfair, then we can't stay as strangers.'

She nodded. 'So what do you have in mind?'

His heart was beating steadily now. 'Let's spend some time together. I think you should move in to the main house. Just until you go back to England,' he said carefully. 'There's plenty of room, and I'm sure your family would feel happier knowing you were being looked after, so let me take care of you. Just for now.'

He waited, watching her face, trying not to let the tension show in his own, and then his heart began to beat with relief and triumph as her eyes met his and she nodded slowly.

CHAPTER SEVEN

'WOULD YOU LIKE some ham, Señora Quested? Or perhaps a couple of eggs?'

Gazing at her already overcrowded plate, Kitty smiled up at the dark-haired woman standing beside her and shook her head. 'No, thank you, Rosa. Honestly, this is perfect.'

She glanced guiltily at the plates of food surrounding her. It all looked delicious, but even if she was eating for two, she wasn't going to make much of a dent in this spread.

Her heart jerked. But perhaps it was not all meant for her? As though following the workings of her brain, Rosa shook her head.

'Señor Zayas always eats breakfast early,' she said, leaning forward to refill Kitty's glass. 'But he told me that he's hoping to join you for lunch.'

'Oh, right.' Her smile felt suddenly cemented to her face. Were her thoughts that obvious? Swallowing her juice, trying to ignore the heat rising over her throat and cheeks, she met Rosa's soft brown eyes. 'Then I'll see him at lunch.'

She had no idea what César had told Rosa about their relationship. Did a man in his position explain the dynamic between himself and a guest to his staff? Probably not. She certainly couldn't imagine him doing it and she certainly wasn't going to try to do so. Not least because right now she wasn't exactly sure how to explain their relationship herself.

They weren't a couple.

But he was the father of her unborn child.

And now they were living together.

She felt a twitch of guilt. Living with César was supposed to reassure her family, and yet now, two days after moving into the main house, she still hadn't told either her parents or Lizzie that she was pregnant or cohabiting with the baby's father.

But how could she? Why *would* she?

Whatever he might have suggested the other day, they both knew it was only a temporary arrangement. At the moment her pregnancy was new and strange, and César felt guilty and responsible, but once she was back in England he would find it easy to move on with his life.

Carefully she laid her knife and fork side by side on the plate. In a way, hadn't that already happened? She might be living under his roof, but she'd barely seen him. They'd been like moons orbiting a planet: occasionally, unavoidably their paths would cross—

But of course she hadn't seen him. Irritably, she pushed aside the disappointment she didn't want or have any right to feel. He was flat-out unpacking his work schedule—*for her.*

Anyway, at least not having him around meant she was free of the disconcerting undercurrent of tension between them. Her throat tightened. She'd tried hard to pretend that it wasn't there, but it was—and that was another reason not to speak to Lizzie.

She needed to get a handle on this confusion she felt for César. Living with him and being pregnant was obviously a big deal, but so what if she was temporarily sharing his home? Or that right now, at least, he wanted to be a part of their baby's life.

Being a parent was a lifelong commitment that needed solid foundations. All they had was one, brief, explosive sexual encounter that meant nothing to either of them.

And, truthfully, it didn't matter how sublime their passion had been, it had nothing to do with the tenderness or the love she'd felt for her husband and nor would it. Because feeling that kind of tenderness and love for someone, anyone—even the father of her child—was not something she was capable of doing any more.

Her skin tightened as she heard the sound of footsteps—heavy, determined, male—in the hallway, and her eyes darted involuntarily towards the door. But the nervous smile that was pulling at her mouth stopped mid-curve as the man glanced briefly into the breakfast room, nodding politely as he walked past.

Her pulse twitched. It was only César's driver—Rodolfo.

Ten minutes later, having finished her breakfast, she found herself standing aimlessly in the soaring entrance hall. Gazing up the stairs, she chewed her lip. She could go up to her room, but that would mean being alone with her thoughts.

Breathing out, she put her hand on the bannister—and then hesitated. Somebody, maybe Rodolfo, had left the door to the terrace open, and she could see two stripes of vivid contrasting blue where the sea met the sky.

It looked temptingly tranquil—unlike her thoughts—

and so, turning away from the stairs, she began walking towards the door.

After weeks of self-imposed imprisonment in the labs it felt good to feel the sun on her face, but soon the lacy clouds would disperse and it would be too hot. She found a path beneath the shade of some tamarind trees and wandered slowly over the heat-baked ground, always aware of the main house at the edge of her vision.

It would be easy to stay out here in the shade, and part of her still shied away from the moment when she would come face to face with César, but maybe that was just what she needed. Spending time with him was the quickest, surest way to see through the glamour and past the passion and so transform him from overheated fantasy into cool reality. After all, no man could be that desirable twenty-four-seven.

She made her way out of the woods that edged the dunes, drawn to the sound of the waves, her face lowered as she scoured the blindingly white sand for pieces of driftwood. She had half an idea for a mobile for the baby—some part of his or her homeland when they were back in England—but for some reason now that she was here on the beach even just the idea of going home made her body tense.

Sighing, she lifted her face, intending to scan the sea instead and instantly her body and brain froze and her stomach went into freefall.

She was not alone.

César was on the beach with a lean, dark-haired man she didn't recognise. And they were fighting, their breathing loud in the still morning air.

Her heart began pounding like a jackhammer.

They were a couple of metres away, moving quickly

and smoothly in the sunlight like water, their bodies bent forward, legs arcing through the air, wrists twisting and fists connecting with skin and bone.

Seconds later her brain stuttered back to life and she felt her pulse slow as she realised that both men were identically dressed in loose white trousers.

So not an actual fight, then, but some kind of sparring session. Only it looked real, and it looked as if they were actually hurting one another. And yet César's face was calm.

She gazed at him, confusion mingling with irritation. What was it about this man that made him so determined to push himself to the limit? Wasn't it enough that he ran a global business? His day-to-day working life held enough risk and drama for most people, but apparently he needed something extra. Rawer. Unrestrained.

Her legs felt suddenly stiff with the effort of tensing them. She needed to move but wanted to hide.

Breathing in, she took a step back and trod heavily on a stick.

It snapped, and the crack echoed like a gunshot across the sand, bouncing off the trees and the water so that both men turned towards her. She caught a swift flash of green as César's eyes locked on hers, widening with surprise, and then sensing weakness, his opponent curved his leg upwards, and her pulse jerked as César was thrown down and landed heavily on the sand.

Kitty blinked. It had all happened so fast.

Just like on the road.

Only this time her legs simply wouldn't move.

She watched mutely as the dark-haired man held out his arm and pulled César to his feet. They exchanged a few words, shook hands, and then César turned and walked towards her, padding across the sand like a mountain lion.

Her heart was beating in her mouth as he stopped in front of her. He was silhouetted black against the sunlight, his features in darkness, but she could feel his gaze all over her. And then he took a step closer, and as he came into focus she was conscious of her sudden audible intake of breath.

He'd clearly been working hard. His trousers were saturated with sweat around the waistband and his body was stippled with beads of perspiration. The ridges of his muscles were sharply defined, and his skin glowed like lacquered gold. She knew her reaction was showing on her face but she couldn't pull her eyes away, and she gazed at him, dry-mouthed, clamping her hands behind her back so as not to give in to an almost overwhelming desire to reach out and pull the draw-cord loose.

Remembering her careless assumption that living with César would strip him of his glamour, she gritted her teeth. Clearly there was a long way to go before that happened.

'You seem to be making a bit of a habit of this,' he said softly.

She swallowed. 'A habit of what?'

He held her gaze. 'Knocking me off my feet.'

Her skin felt warm. There was a shimmering tension in the air, low and taut, like the hum of an audience waiting for a play to start. Not touching him was an actual test of willpower like not scratching a mosquito bite.

Startled by the strength of her desire, she cleared her throat and said, 'I didn't knock you off your feet. I was over here, minding my own business. You just weren't paying attention.'

He laughed. 'That's pretty much what Oscar just said to me.'

Her heart stumbled against her ribs. Being around César was supposed to be a sobering reality check, but when his mouth turned up at the corners like that, with the sunlight glittering in his eyes, he was irresistible.

'Oscar?' She was trying to control her voice, but she could hear the catch of nervousness.

'My instructor.'

Glancing past him, she breathed out. 'So, what is he teaching you?' Part of her was really interested, but mainly she was just grateful to break away from his deep, green gaze.

'It's called Eskrima. It's a martial art. Shall we...?'

He gestured towards the house and they began walking back up the beach. It was easier talking to him sideways. For starters, she wasn't having to deal with the continuing shock of his beauty, but also the conversation seemed to flow more naturally with each step.

'Is it Cuban?'

He shook his head. 'It comes from the Philippines. I was spending quite a lot of time down there a couple of years ago.' His eyes met hers. 'They drink a lot of rum there.'

'Yes, it's the third largest market in the world.' She matched his easy smile with a small, tight one of her own. 'They have their own brands, don't they? Lizzie and Bill went on holiday there last year, and they brought me back a bottle. It was a limited edition.' She hesitated, groping for a memory of how it had tasted. 'It was dark...quite oaky.'

'Yeah, they char the barrels.' He frowned. 'Sorry, I didn't mean to get sidetracked into talking about work. Basically, when I was there my regular personal trainer, Félix, had an accident, and he recommended Oscar. And Oscar is a Lakan—a black belt in Eskrima.'

He broke off and glanced up, his attention snagged by a low rumble overhead. Her gaze following his, she watched a dark green plane cut through the cloudless blue sky on its way to the US military base at Guantánamo Bay. As it disappeared from view she looked back down and instantly wished she hadn't. He was looking at her intently, and suddenly her hands were trembling.

'I spoke to the clinic.' His voice sounded harsh against the waves. 'They've arranged a scan for this morning and then we'll see Dr Moreno.'

She blinked. 'Oh, okay…'

'Apparently it's to date the pregnancy.'

His eyes were steady, his expression neutral, but she felt a defensive jolt shoot through her. Although had she really thought that a man like him would simply accept her word?

She felt a sudden hot rush of tears, and in an instant her mood flipped.

In the five years since Jimmy's death she'd worked hard to find some kind of peace and equilibrium, only since meeting César she'd felt like a ship at sea, pushed and pulled in every direction by emotional currents and riptides. Emotions she couldn't control. Emotions she didn't understand.

And it wasn't just hormones, she thought with a burst of irrational anger. It was *his* fault she was feeling like this. His fault she was feeling so conflicted. His fault she was remembering how it felt to want someone, and need them. Only she wasn't supposed to feel like that for this handsome stranger.

If only this was Jimmy's baby it would all be so much simpler...

'Kitty—'

She knew her expression must have changed, and that he'd noticed. She could hear it in his voice. But, striving to keep her own voice on an even keel, she cut him off. 'What time is the scan?'

He stared at her, and for a few half-seconds she thought he was going to rewind the conversation, but after a brief silence he said, 'Eleven o'clock.'

'Okay. I'll be ready.' They were inside the house now, and she glanced pointedly upstairs. 'I'm feeling a little tired, so I'm going to go and have a lie-down.'

He stepped back. 'Then I'll let you go. I'll see you at eleven.'

And, turning, he walked away from her towards the kitchen.

She watched him disappear. If he had turned he would have seen the way her eyes followed him. But he didn't turn and, feeling a stab of betrayal that was as baffling as it was painful, she turned and began climbing up the stairs.

Kitty was relieved to discover that the clinic César had chosen looked more like an upmarket hotel than a private hospital. In the car on the way over she had been tense, her stomach knotting as memories of the numerous trips she'd made to hospital with Jimmy kept floating into her mind, but the foyer was clean and modern, and the smiling staff were dressed to match the decor in varying shades of taupe and cream.

And now she was lying on a bed, her bare stomach covered in gel, as the female sonographer moved the probe over her skin, tilting it from one side to the other, her eyes fixed on the screen in front of her.

'There we are,' she said quietly. 'There's your baby.'

Kitty glanced up at the screen and felt her heart contract. The sonographer spoke very good English, which was lucky. Because had she been speaking Spanish, it would have been easy for her to think that something had got lost in translation.

Her breathing was suddenly out of time. She could hardly believe it. The baby was tiny, but it was real. She really was pregnant. It was extraordinary, impossible, miraculous. But, like all real miracles, it was undeniable.

'And this is the head...that's a leg and a foot...and that's the heartbeat.'

The sonographer was smiling at her and she smiled back dazedly. She'd held that positive test in her hand, but up until this moment she hadn't believed it was actually happening, hadn't wanted to believe it was true for fear of disappointment. But it was true. Finally it had happened. And she felt so blissfully and unconditionally happy that it was as though her whole body was filled with light.

'Is everything okay?' she said quietly.

The other woman nodded.

'Baby's CRL is just under three centimetres, so I think we're looking at about nine weeks. When you see Dr Moreno you can discuss booking a second scan. We'll be able to see a lot more detail then, but right now everything looks great. Now, I'm guessing you'll want a photo?'

Kitty found her voice. 'Yes, please—and thank you.'

Her eyes found César. Since shaking hands with the sonographer he hadn't said a word, but she had expected him to echo her thanks, to see a reciprocal joy on his face. Only he didn't speak. He just kept staring at the screen, his expression intense, his eyes fixed on the shifting image.

She was about to prompt him when a low but distinctive buzzing filled the small room.

'Sorry, I need to take this.'

He didn't sound sorry and, glancing over, she saw that he didn't look it either.

Pulling out his phone, he stood up. 'Excuse me. José, *gracias por llamarme...*'

Watching the door close behind him, she felt a slippery rush of panic. She'd pictured this moment inside her head so many times in the past, and it wasn't supposed to look like this.

Her heart was suddenly too big for her chest. But why had she ever thought this would work with him? She didn't know this man, so how could she begin to know how he would react to anything? More importantly, how could she expect to bring up a child with him?

Picking up his coffee cup, César glanced at the darkening sky. The air was hot and sticky. It was going to rain—and it needed to rain to break the tension in the air.

Jaw tightening, his eyes flickered over to where Kitty sat on the other side of the table, her grey gaze fixed on the horizon. If only the rain could also ease the tension between them.

After the scan they had driven to his sugar cane plantation for lunch. He'd told himself that he needed to speak to his estate manager, José Luis, in person, and he'd told Kitty that he wanted to show her a part of Cuba she hadn't seen. But the truth was that he had simply needed an excuse to drive somewhere—to have an actual, achievable destination in one area of his life.

He took a mouthful of coffee. Since leaving the clinic he'd been trying to think it through logically—but no matter that he had a picture of his as yet unborn son or daughter tucked in his jacket pocket, he still couldn't imagine being a father in just under seven months.

Glancing up, he felt his pulse accelerate as he caught sight of his reflection in the veranda window.

You don't need to imagine it, he told himself, remembering that tiny heart squeezing rhythmically on the screen. *Just take a good look at yourself because it's already happened. You are a father.*

A father?

Even just thinking it was like being hit by a truck. It was ridiculous. He wasn't in a relationship, he wasn't qualified, and he certainly wasn't ready—

His face stiffened.

Ready? Just as he hadn't been ready to take over the business?

He felt a familiar rush of shame and regret. When his father had sat him down and told him that it was time for him to step up he hadn't refused outright, but his stunned silence had been enough of an answer, and with a little persuasion from his mother his father had acquiesced to his plea for 'just one more year'.

And it had been the biggest mistake of his life.

He'd been like some puppy, let off the leash for the first time, rushing up to greet each and every stranger like a long-lost friend. No wonder Celia had found it so easy to string him along. The further she'd thrown the stick, the faster he'd had run to catch it and give it back to her. Except he hadn't given her a stick, but a ring. And not any old ring either, but his grandmother's engagement ring.

Blotting out the memory, his hands gripped the coffee cup more tightly. It didn't matter if he wasn't ready. There was no question of him not stepping up this time. How could there be?

It might be a future he hadn't imagined, but this was his child, and he had meant what he'd said to Kitty. He wanted to make this work. He wanted to marry her. And he'd thought —hoped—that the scan, that seeing their baby together, might nudge her towards changing her mind.

His eyes flickered across to where she sat beside him, silent and still. But instead she had retreated further, and it was his fault.

He knew his silence had hurt her, and he knew he shouldn't have taken that phone call. But he'd had no words—or none eloquent or poetic enough to express the swelling tangle of his feelings on seeing his baby's heartbeat. Not to voice the fear or the wonder, and certainly not the fiercely protective urge he'd felt deep in his guts, not just for the baby but for Kitty too.

There had been no filter, no shield to protect himself, and he'd felt horribly exposed. So when he'd felt her gaze on his face he'd ignored it, not wanting to take on the intimacy of that shared moment and all that it implied.

But that baby growing inside her was so much more than just a baby.

It was a test.

A test that so far he'd failed.

He might have succeeded in getting Kitty to live under his roof, but how was he supposed to present that to his parents? They would be confused and disappointed. *Again*.

No, he needed to marry Kitty—only right now she was barely talking to him.

He gritted his teeth. Actually, he had a strong suspicion that she was ignoring him, but what was he supposed to do?

He didn't coax women or chase after them. Not since Celia. Not since he'd made a fool of himself. It had been the first and only time in his life he had felt helpless and exposed, and he didn't want to feel like that ever again. So, even though he hated letting fear dictate his actions, he'd set up his life so he would never have to feel that way with any other woman.

So that he could always walk away.

Only he couldn't walk away this time.

He breathed out unsteadily. He didn't want to walk away this time. Or at least, not alone.

Pushing back his chair, he stood up. 'Let's go for a walk.' She stared at him warily and, breathing slowly, he held out his hand. 'Please, would you come for a walk with me?'

He watched her face, seeing the conflict, the uncertainty, and then finally she nodded.

They walked slowly, side by side. Behind them jagged green mountains rose up to meet the brilliant blue sky and lush vegetation crowded the path, purple and pink flowers speckling the dark leafy foliage like stars in the night sky.

She was wearing the same dress she'd worn the other

day, and its simplicity combined with her loose hair gave her a breakable quality.

'How are you feeling?'

She stared up at him. 'Fine. Just a little tired, really. It's probably the heat.'

He studied her face. Her cheeks were flushed, just as they had been when she'd kissed him in the club—and, feeling his body respond to the memory of where such a kiss could lead, he gritted his teeth.

Persuading Kitty to move in with him had been a compromise—a first step towards getting her to change her mind about marrying him. Only he was starting to wonder if it had been a good idea after all. Being around her was torment enough, but after the passion they'd shared this awkward formality was like a slap in the face.

Pushing aside his frustration, he glanced up at the sky. 'It'll rain soon, and then it'll be cooler. Or we could take a shower. There's a waterfall just down here.'

He held back some overhanging branches and Kitty brushed past him. He heard her soft intake of breath and tucked it away, gratified by her reaction but not quite ready to admit how gratified.

He stared at the waterfall, trying to picture it through her eyes, to feel her wonder as she gazed at the low outcrop of rock and the gentle cascade of water tumbling into the shimmering sapphire pool.

'It's beautiful. So, is this part of your business empire?' Her eyes were clear and grey, but she looked more nervous than curious.

He shrugged. 'In a way. Obviously the business needs cane, and I like knowing the provenance of my raw materials, but having all of this lets me play at being a farmer.' A drop of rain hit the water, then another, and another.

'Here, take my hand.' He led her up to where the rocks overhung the clear turquoise water. 'We can wait here.' He took a breath. 'And while we're waiting we can talk about what happens next.'

Her expression shifted minutely, her mouth stiffening. 'I thought this was what happened next.' She spoke carefully, as though she was confirming a booking at a hotel or restaurant.

'It was, but now that we've had the scan I thought we should think about what we want to tell our families.' He wasn't going to demand that they marry—not after what had happened last time—but their living together hadn't answered all the questions raised by the pregnancy.

There was a silence, and then she cleared her throat. 'The truth, I suppose.' She bit her lip.

He felt his eyebrows draw together in a frown. He'd assumed that she'd already rung her home, but clearly she hadn't. That surprised him, and it stung too—more than he cared to admit.

'Don't you want to tell your family?'

'I do…it's just that I don't know how to tell them.' Her voice was taut, stretched tight like the string of a kite.

'Are you worried they're going to be upset?'

She looked up at him, her grey eyes wide with confusion. '*Upset?* No, of course not.' Her voice was shaking. 'They'll be delighted…' She hesitated. 'They know how much I wanted to get pregnant…how long Jimmy and I tried. All they want is for me to be happy.'

'So what's the problem?' He paused, remembering her shuttered expression when he'd talked to her on the beach. 'Look, I know how it must have sounded earlier, but I'm not questioning my paternity. That's not why I arranged the scan. In fact, I didn't arrange it. The clinic suggested it and I thought it was standard.'

'I know.' She lowered her head. 'It's not you.'

César took a breath. He was caught between the need to know more and the need to keep his distance, but if he wanted to keep his distance then why was he even here? If he'd meant what he'd said then, whatever this was, he couldn't leave her to deal with it alone.

His mind inched forward and then stopped, teetering on the edge of a new and previously unconsidered outcome. 'I thought you said you didn't have any regrets. Have you changed your mind? About the baby?'

He spoke calmly, but he felt pain saying the words out loud—a pain that was equalled by his relief as she shook her head.

'No—no!'

She looked up, her eyes wide with shock and denial, and he could hear the strain at the edges of her voice.

'I want this baby.'

Her shoulders hunched, and he stared down at her, then slowly reached out and took her hand. He wanted to help, or at least to understand.

'So what's the problem?'

'*That's* the problem.' She pressed her knuckles against her mouth. 'I wanted a baby for so long, for Jimmy, for us, only now I'm pregnant and he's not here. And I should be miserable, but I'm not.'

She looked up him, her distress so undisguised that it hurt to look at her.

'Kitty, it's okay.'

Watching her attempt to control her tears was worse

than seeing her actually cry. Unpeeling her hand from her mouth, he pulled her closer.

'Look, you're putting too much pressure on yourself.'

His fingers tightened around hers. Celia's tears had been meaningless, manufactured on demand to manipulate his emotions, and normally if a woman cried he wanted to leave. But Kitty's pain was raw and real, and her grief transcended his need...his wish to stay emotionally detached.

And so what if it did? He was only doing what he did every day as CEO of a global business. Doing what he did best: staying calm, making things happen, finding solutions. And in this case that meant holding Kitty's hand and being strong for her.

'This is all new and confusing, but it's okay to be happy about the baby.'

Her eyes were bright. 'And I *am* happy—I'm so happy. But I just feel so guilty.'

Guilty. The word resonated inside his head as he stroked her back. He knew all about feeling guilty. Guilt had driven his life, overriding all other impulses, good and bad, and changing him into this guarded island—an emotionally autonomous man focused on work.

But his guilt was penance. Kitty's was undeserved.

'For what?'

She hesitated.

'For what?' he asked again. 'For carrying on? For having a future?'

She shook her head. 'I wish it was that. That's what I should be feeling—and I did at first. I want to feel it now, but all I can think about is you. And what happened with you.'

His body tensed as he braced against the memory of

that moment. The spray from the waterfall was warm, but not as warm as the heat licking his stomach—a heat that had nothing to do with his memories and everything to do with the woman holding his hand.

'You shouldn't feel guilty about that.'

He was close enough to see the scattering of freckles along her cheekbones and the pulse working at the base of her throat. His body tightened with need.

'I don't. I feel guilty for wanting it to happen again.' Her free hand bunched the fabric of her dress. 'I don't know why I feel like this...' she whispered.

His body stilled, mirroring the tension in hers. 'I'm not sure if that's a compliment or not,' he said carefully.

She bit her lip. 'I wasn't expecting anything to happen—and then, when it did, I thought it was because I was here and because it's been so long since there was anyone...so long since I even wanted anyone. Only it wasn't that. It isn't—'

His breathing stilled. In her villa, he'd wanted her in the moment. He could still remember the intensity of his desire and, more erotically, of hers—the swell of blood, the heat, the way her body had fitted against his.

Now, though, in the face of her honesty, he could admit that it hadn't been enough. That even as he'd turned and walked away he had been craving more, and it was a need that wasn't diminishing.

Need.

The word made his heart beat faster. But why? He wasn't talking about emotional entanglement and neither was she. He was talking about lust. Sex. Desire. An elemental, physical yearning like hunger or thirst.

He shifted just a fraction, feeling the slight swell of her stomach. But this baby—their baby—was a connection that went beyond mere lust. They were bound by DNA now, and that was bigger than both of them, so he didn't have to fight this—just accept it.

She breathed out unevenly and, heart pounding, he stared into her eyes, mesmerised by the longing he saw there…a longing he knew was mirrored in his own green gaze.

He felt a spinning sensation, almost as though he was drunk. In a way he was…drunk on the realisation that he was just a man, and she was just a woman, and they were equal. Equal in their need and their want. And by giving in to that want he would let go of the mistake he'd made and the fear that he'd let control his life for so long. For *too* long.

'I want you,' he said softly. 'And I haven't stopped wanting you since I walked out of your front door all those weeks ago. It's not wrong or right—it just *is*.' He touched her face, brushing his thumb over her bottom lip, exulting in the feel of her skin, the heat of her breath. 'I can't fight this any more. I don't want to fight it.'

She took a deep breath. 'I don't want to fight it either.'

His blood felt like air in his veins as she leaned forward and flicked her tongue over his lips—and then, threading his hand through her hair, his mouth seeking hers, he kissed her fiercely.

CHAPTER EIGHT

THE SOUND OF the water was rushing in time with her breath.

Inching backwards, she stared up at him dazedly. Her head was swimming, and nothing seemed to matter except his taut profile and the urgent, hungry beat of her heart.

'Your jacket...' she whispered. 'It's getting wet.'

'So is your dress.' His voice was hoarse.

Her throat was dry. 'Then help me take it off.'

They reached out for one another, his hand locking in her hair as she grabbed at his shirt, their mouths colliding as they kissed hungrily, tongues probing, lips bruising.

He groaned into her mouth and they broke apart, panting.

'I've been thinking about this for weeks.' His eyes, fiercely green, burned into hers.

'So have I,' she whispered.

His face was taut and she could see the muscles in his arms tensing, as though he was having to hold himself in check. She felt a rush of blood, hot and sudden, at the hunger in his gaze.

'So what are you waiting for?'

His eyes were trained on her face. 'The baby. Is it okay to—? I don't want to hurt you.'

She slid off her sandals, reached out and touched his chest. 'You won't.'

Her head was spinning, her pulse racing. She felt as though she was melting. She wanted him so badly—wanted him as she had never wanted anything or anyone…ever. And this wasn't about some fantasy. This was real. And it was what they both wanted. That was all that mattered.

Reaching up, she slid her hands beneath his shirt, shaking with the freedom of being able to touch him and the relief that she didn't have to stop—that he didn't want her to stop. She clutched at his shoulders, pushing her tongue into his warm mouth as they moved as one, stepping into the shallow water, circling through shafts of raindrops, bodies pressing together in time to the beating of their hearts.

She touched his collar, fumbled impatiently with his tie, her fingers plucking at the knot, jerking it loose, then tugging at the buttons of his shirt.

As her hands touched his warm, bare skin her breath stalled for a moment and she stepped back on legs that shook unsteadily. He was gorgeous, more gorgeous than any man should be allowed to be, and whatever her memory had conjured up the reality outdid any fantasy. He was crazily, stupidly beautiful—all lean, defined muscles and olive skin that was smooth aside from the line of fine dark hair that ran down the centre of his abs, thickening as it disappeared beneath the waistband of his trousers.

Heart pounding, she slid her hands lightly over his chest and, standing on tiptoe, kissed him again gently, delicately, tasting him as she would one of his rums.

He grunted, tugged off his shirt and dropped it, and then, reaching out, he looped his fingers under the thin straps of her dress and slid them over her shoulders, peeling the damp fabric from her overheated skin. She felt it slide over her body and pool at her feet. She wasn't wearing a bra, and above the soft rush of the water she heard him swallow, saw his control snap, sensed the tension in his arms loosen like a spring uncoiling.

'You're beautiful,' he said hoarsely, 'so beautiful.'

He breathed out raggedly and for a moment he just stared at her, his eyes dark and sightless. Her nipples hardened beneath his gaze—and then she sucked in a breath as he reached out and began to stroke them with the palm of his hand.

It was too much. They were too sensitive to touch.

She grabbed his fingers. 'Not there,' she whispered. 'Here.' She pulled his hand lower, pressing it against the ache between her thighs.

He shifted against her, his leg moving between hers, and she felt the hard length of him pushing against her. Only it was not enough. Her hands trembled. She wanted all of him. She wanted—*needed*—everything he had to give.

Her hands moved to his waist, and then to where the force of his desire pressed against his trousers, her pulse jerking as she began tugging at his belt, working the leather through the buckle.

As he breathed out unsteadily her nerves were forgotten and she felt a rush of excitement. His green eyes were fierce and filled with hunger, and she knew that he was fighting for control.

Knowing that he wanted her as much as she wanted him made her feel powerful in a way she had never felt before, and suddenly she wanted to test that power. Holding his gaze, she reached out and rested her hand against the thickness of his arousal.

He let out a hiss of air.

Shaking his head, he swore in Spanish. And then his hands closed around her wrists and he pulled them behind her back. Bending his head, he took her mouth again. Her insides felt hot and tight and she squirmed closer, raising her hips, seeking to ease the pulsing ache between her thighs. But he was holding her still, keeping himself just out of reach.

Her stomach tensed and she moaned in frustration as he wrenched his mouth away. His eyes were trained on her face. For a moment he just stared at her, and then, holding both of her wrists in one hand, he pulled her forward so that the warm spray trickled over her bare skin.

Her heart began to thump as he leaned forward and ran his fingers slowly over her breasts and belly, then lower to the triangle of her panties. As he slid his hand beneath the fabric her stomach flipped over and inside out with need and frustration, and she arched her aching body up towards his, wanting more, *needing* more.

'Please...' she whispered.

He dropped to his knees and she felt an arrow of heat, sharp and low, as he hooked a finger into one side of her panties and tugged gently, drawing them down her legs and tossing them away.

Her nipples tightened painfully. She felt as though she was teetering on the edge of a bottomless drop. A pulse was beating relentlessly between her thighs— and then his tongue pushed between the damp curls and she gasped.

The rain was pounding down now, fat droplets exploding on the rocks behind them, blotting out her heartbeat and his ragged breathing.

Her body was opening out with longing and she was shaking with need, her whole body trembling. A fluttering heat was spreading out from his tongue, growing stronger, more urgent, impossible to ignore. She could feel herself slipping away, the beat of her desire out of sync with her throbbing heartbeat.

Oh, she had never felt like this before. This need was raw and imperative. It felt like water, or air, or sunlight and she could think of nothing other than the tip of his tongue…steady, precise, teasing, merciless.

Her body was screaming now and, tugging her hands free, she grabbed his hair, her fingers biting into his scalp, pulling him closer, opening herself to him as heat exploded in her pelvis.

She breathed out unsteadily as César kissed his way up her body, chasing the aftershocks quivering over her skin. Her hands were still grabbing his skin, clutching and tensing—and then her fingers found the zip of his trousers.

He groaned as she freed him, and she watched his face tighten with concentration as he held himself back from his own release. Curving his fingers under her bottom, he lifted her up so that he could ease her on to his body.

She began to rock against him, her head spinning, and he wrapped his hands around her hips and pulled her closer, his hunger accelerating. Reaching up, he brought her face down and kissed her fiercely and then, gripping her waist, he pushed up inside her. Instantly, she began to move more urgently, breath quickening. His hips were meeting hers…

'*Yes.*' Her lips parted against his mouth. '*Yes...
Yes...*' she whispered.

He breathed in sharply, jerking his mouth away from
hers. Muscles clenching, blood hardening to iron, he
thrust into her, burying his face against her neck to stop
himself crying out. He held her close, and then, easing
himself free, he backed her gently against the wall of
rock, leaning forward to shield her body with his.

Kitty was still trying to catch her breath. He was
calm and solid beside her, his muscles relaxed, his arms
holding her against him, supporting her flushed, shaken
body.

Had they really just done that? Had *she* really just
done that? Was it her hormones? Or was it this place?

She glanced over his shoulder at the lush greenery
and brightly coloured butterflies. It was all so wild and
vibrant—like stepping into some primitive landscape.
Was that why she'd lost all sense of who she was? All
her inhibitions?

But she knew that it was none of those things. It was
him. And her. The two of them together.

Burying her face against his burning damp skin, she
felt the reality of what had just happened overwhelm
her. It had been so fierce, so urgent, so quick. One spark
was all it had taken: her body the flint to his steel.

For a moment she couldn't bring herself to move or
speak, and perhaps he felt the same way—because he
kept his cheek against her face, his breath, still rapid
and unsteady, in her hair.

She leaned into him, enjoying the sensation of his
skin against hers, the warmth of his body and the steady
beat of his heart. She felt fearless: he had *made* her feel
fearless. Even her nakedness felt natural. His body fit-

ted hers with a symmetry that felt predetermined, as though once upon a time they had been joined and then separated, and she wondered why she had fought against this moment.

But it couldn't last for ever.

She pushed at him gently and their eyes met. Scared of what she might see, she looked down to where her fingers were splayed against his chest. She blinked. In the heat of passion she'd barely registered the scars, but now she stared at them intently. They were of differing lengths, some thin and white, one darker and ridged.

'Did you get that one riding your bike?' She ran her fingertip over the puckered skin.

He nodded. 'I hit a bump in the road, came off, and the bike caught me in the chest.'

'And this?' She touched his side.

His eyes were opaque in the sunlight. 'I was climbing and I missed a foothold. I dropped about a hundred feet before the rope caught me, and I got scraped against the rock.'

A hundred feet. 'What happened?'

He shrugged. 'I chalked up my hands and carried on.'

She couldn't think of anything to say to that. But she didn't need to. He was already reaching down to pick up her dress.

They got dressed with difficulty, their wet clothes twisting and tightening against their skin, and then they walked back to the house, not holding hands but not tensing or leaping apart when their fingers brushed together either.

'I don't how that happened,' he murmured.

Looking up into his eyes, she gave him a quick, shy smile and he grinned sheepishly. Around them rainbows danced in the sunlight, taking form in the spray-soaked air.

'I just meant I didn't plan it.' His face was serious, intent, shocked. 'I don't normally act like this, but I've never wanted any woman the way I want you.' His eyes dropped to her throat and, lowering his mouth, he pressed his lips against the tiny beating pulse there. 'Something happens when I'm around you... I feel so frantic.'

'I know.' She pressed her hand against his chest, feeling his heart throb against her fingers. 'I feel the same way. And I didn't plan it either.'

'Was it okay? I wasn't too rough—?'

Looking up into his face, she could see the concern in his green eyes. She shook her head. 'No, you weren't rough. It was wonderful.'

'Wonderful' didn't really do justice to what they'd just shared. It had been sublime. And César was so gorgeous it was no wonder that she'd clawed off his clothes in broad daylight like a ravenous animal. Or that she would gladly do it all again.

But however handsome or sexy César was, that was irrelevant to their future. Her heart was not for the taking and marriage was still not an option.

She felt her stomach tighten. But neither was pretending that something wasn't happening between them: it was. And it wasn't just sex.

But why did it have to be a binary choice between sex and marriage? Was there no room for something in between? Something bespoke—just for them. After all, it was the twenty-first century.

She thought back to César's scars. This was a man who took risks and tested his limits. She, on the other hand...

It wasn't that she hadn't experienced anything in her life. She had: love, marriage, sickness and death. That was a lot more than most twenty-seven-year-olds. Only that was the problem. It had all been too much, too quickly. She had felt passive, powerless, like a passenger in a speeding car.

But César made her feel powerful. She might not want to skydive or free climb, but knowing how she affected him made her feel in control and euphoric in the same way. Plus, whatever happened, they were both parents to this baby growing inside her.

And all that seemed to matter more than trying to classify their relationship status.

Only did he feel the same way?

His hand reached for hers and he stopped beside her. 'Kitty, I've been thinking. About us. About what we're doing. I've been thinking that I'd like it to carry on.'

Watching her eyes widen, he reached out and pushed a curl away from her forehead.

'I don't mean what happened by the waterfall specifically—although that was incredible...'

He smiled, and the slow burn of his gaze made her nipples tighten painfully.

'So, what *are* you suggesting?'

His eyes rested on her face—not just green but gold and amber, like pirate treasure.

'Look, I'm not ready to go back to Havana yet. I haven't had a proper break in a long time, so how do you feel about staying on here for a couple of days?'

Her heart was hammering in her chest. 'I think it sounds like a lovely idea, but I've already taken quite a lot of time off.'

He shook his head slowly. 'You don't need to worry

about that, I spoke to the big boss—he's a great guy, by the way, cool and good-looking and charming—and he said that you can take as much time as you want.'

She bit her lip, trying to stop the smile that was tugging at her mouth.

Sensing her indecision, he reached out and, taking her hand, pulled her closer. 'Please, Kitty. I know I've juggled my schedule, but it's not enough. I owe it to you and the baby to take a step back from the business and not just relocate my office to my home.'

Lifting her chin, she met his gaze. 'And that means what?'

'I don't know.'

The honesty of his answer caught her off guard.

He hesitated. 'I can't in all honesty say that sex hasn't got something to do with it,' he said carefully. 'But it's not the only reason I want to spend time with you. We're going to have a baby…our lives are going to be overlapping for a long time.'

She nodded. 'I know.'

Leaning forward, he kissed her mouth lightly, brushing his lips against hers so that her pulse jumped in her throat.

'That's why I think we should stop pretending. I want you and you want me and there's nothing wrong in us feeling that way—so why act like there is? I know what we have isn't conventional, but that doesn't mean it has to be complicated,' he said quietly. 'We can just keep everything nice and simple.'

She felt his gaze on his face. For a second their eyes were level as they breathed in one another's scent. Who could resist what he was offering? Pure pleasure with no catch. And it was what she wanted too.

Reaching up, she stroked his face. 'I'd like that.'

His eyes were dark with hunger, a hunger that reflected her own, and her body was already starting to melt as he lowered his face to hers and kissed her fiercely.

Mornings had definitely improved, César thought as he leaned back against the pillow.

Three days had passed since their frenzied encounter by the waterfall and the moment when he and Kitty had agreed to stay on at the plantation, and he was lying in bed—the bed he now shared with Kitty—watching her get dressed.

His gaze followed her fingers as they lingered over the buttons of her blouse. For some inexplicable reason he found it incredibly erotic—inexplicable because she was buttoning it up, not unbuttoning it.

But there was something about her focus, the small furrow of concentration in her forehead, that made heat shimmy over his skin. Or maybe it was the way her freshly showered hair was scattering droplets of water onto the fabric, so that he could see her bare skin through the white cotton.

Was it really only three days? Actually it was three days and two nights of pure, blissful pleasure. And yet in some ways it felt as though she had always been a part of his life.

He wasn't complaining. Heat churned in his stomach as he rewound that morning. They'd made love twice—first with the feverish hunger that had characterised their first encounter, and then again more slowly, touching, tasting, exploring each other's bodies.

He couldn't remember wanting a woman so badly, or a time when sex had held such power over him.

Even with Celia.

Now that he could compare her to Kitty, he could see that she had been a youthful infatuation. He'd been a spoilt, handsome young man, used to girls chasing him, and she'd played hard to get. That had been what had really got him hooked. Had she chased him, or responded to his advances, he would not have been so obsessively determined to win her.

But it felt strange to be so fixated on one woman now, given that he'd spent most of his adult life pursuing variety, not commitment. He'd assumed that his fascination for Kitty lay in her unattainability, but now they were having sex and yet nothing had changed. He still couldn't stop thinking about her.

He shifted beneath the sheet, then instantly regretted it; the smooth fabric brushing against his skin was an agonizing reminder of her teasing touch.

But with an eager, responsive Kitty in his bed, it was hardly surprising he was distracted. After so long just fulfilling basic physical hunger, it was a novelty to want someone specifically and repeatedly, to indulge in her feverish touch, to look forward to seeing her.

He felt his spine tense. And, of course, looking forward to seeing someone was natural for lovers—perhaps even more so for lovers who didn't love one another.

And he didn't love Kitty.

But he did want to marry her.

And when it happened—and it *would* happen—it would work for both of them. He would offer her security and the kind of lifestyle she could only dream about for their child, and marriage to her would allow him to present his parents with the 'happy-ever-after' ending they wanted for him.

Or so it would appear, and that was all he needed it to do.

His hand tightened around the edge of the sheet.

He told himself that he was simply being pragmatic. Believing in love as a prerequisite for marriage was a nice idea—but if love and marriage went together like the proverbial horse and carriage why were there so many divorces?

But there was more to his reasoning than just cynicism. The truth was—and it killed him to admit it, even privately—that mostly it was fear. Fear of what would happen if he repeated the mistake he'd made with Celia and allowed himself to muddle lust, or in this case lust and duty, with love.

Kitty turned and gazed down at him, her eyes flaring as they connected with his bare upper body, so that he felt his groin harden.

Why think about any of that anyway? Right now, with access to her delectable body, he was not so much happy as willing to let her set the pace. Rather than pressurising her to change her mind, he was prepared to play a long-ish game—and that meant not just focusing on the present, but laying the foundations for the future and accepting that, for the moment at least, this arrangement was a jump-off point for the next step.

Tipping her head to one side, Kitty scooped up her mass of hair and raised her arms. It was mid-afternoon, the hottest time of the day, and she was sprawled on one of the loungers that were dotted invitingly around the veranda. She'd just detected the slightest of breezes and she let out a long, slow breath. The quiver of air felt blissfully cool against her neck.

Actually, thanks to César, she felt blissful all over.

She stretched out against the cushions, enjoying the ache in the limbs and the sated heaviness of her body. Oscar Wilde had been wrong. Giving in to temptation was not making César any less desirable. On the contrary, every kiss seemed only to intensify her hunger for him, and her pleasure—endless and exhilarating, mindless and insatiable—was nothing like it had ever been before.

She let go of her hair, feeling it cascade over her shoulders.

Nothing like it had been with Jimmy.

But how could she think that sex with César was better than with the man she'd loved and married and watched die?

Her heartbeat slowed, and she waited for the pang of guilt. Only none came. Was she then starting to realise that it was impossible to compare these two men? Or those two versions of herself?

She had never kissed Jimmy as they'd sat down for lunch and then forgotten all about the meal, abandoning the food on her plate in the heat of a different kind of abandonment.

But with Jimmy she had been so young, and in love for the first time. They had both been inexpert, nervous, but at the same time everything had been so familiar. There had never been that spark of hunger, nor any stomach-swooping rush of need because they—and everyone else—had always expected it to happen.

With César she was learning that there was a lot more to sex—and to herself. She was discovering a hot, passionate woman who was living in the moment and enjoying it.

From somewhere inside the house she heard César's voice. He was on the phone and, judging by the mix of affection and exasperation in his voice, she was willing to bet that either he was speaking to his mother or his father.

Picking up her robe, she sat up and tugged it over her bikini. He'd talked about his family, but people were different when they talked *to* their family. Standing up, curious to catch a glimpse of this uncensored version of César, she walked quietly back into the house.

He was wearing his usual dark suit, talking in Spanish, and she allowed herself a moment to enjoy the flow of his words. It was such a romantic-sounding language.

Her chest tightened. Except that César's responses were growing curter by the minute.

Abruptly he hung up and, not wanting to look like an eavesdropper, she said quickly, 'Hi, I was just going to go upstairs and get changed—'

'Okay.'

Crossing the room, he picked up a cup of coffee and drank it swiftly. She stared after him uncertainly. He seemed tense and upset, more so than she'd ever seen him. Except when she'd refused to marry him.

'Who was that on the phone?'

He turned, his green eyes wary. 'My father.'

'Is everything okay?'

He frowned. 'He's fine. He's just annoyed.'

His face didn't change but his voice sounded clipped, distant—the voice of a CEO talking to an employee.

'About what?'

He frowned, glancing away. 'Nothing. It's not important.'

'So why are you upset?'

'Why do you care?'

She stared at him, dumbfounded, winded by the harshness in the voice and by the realisation that this was how he saw her. She might be in his bed and carrying his child, but his thoughts were off-limits.

Avoiding his cool, green gaze, she breathed out unsteadily. 'You seemed upset. I just wanted to h-help.' She stumbled over the word.

'Kitty, please. I'm sorry.' His voice had changed, the harshness fading. 'I shouldn't have said that.' Reaching out, he took her hand, his eyes soft now, contrite. 'I was angry. With my father. Only I took it out on you.' His jaw tensed. 'I don't even know why I said anything. I knew he'd get mad.'

'What did you say?'

'I told him I was thinking about climbing El Capitan.' Catching sight of her baffled expression, he said, 'It's a nine-hundred-metre granite slab. In Yosemite.'

Thinking about his scars, she felt her heart do some kind of complicated two-step against her ribs. 'Your dad's probably just worried about you.'

'Probably.' His forehead creased. 'He can't understand why I'd want to do something like that.'

Kitty stared at him. 'And why do you?'

Now he was staring at her—only she got the sense that he wasn't seeing her, but someone else. Maybe the question had never occurred to him. Probably it hadn't, given that he appeared to divert all his non-work-based energies into riding motorbikes and climbing ridiculously high pieces of rock.

'I don't know.' He shrugged. 'My life is pretty full-on. Sometimes—a lot of the time—it's difficult to switch off. But when you're on a motorbike, or climb-

ing without a rope, the consequences of making a error
are so stark you have to concentrate completely, and it's
kind of peaceful.'

Peaceful? How could hanging onto a rock face be
in any way peaceful?

He gave her a small, tight smile. 'I know it sounds
crazy, but time seems to slow right down. Everything
disappears. You're just in the moment and it's like
you're dancing with the rock. And when you reach the
summit you have this euphoria…'

She nodded, but her hand crept over her stomach.
How could anything or anyone compete with that? 'It
sounds incredible.'

He paused as though he was hunting for words or
trying to make a decision. She caught sight of the wariness in his eyes and she waited, half expecting him to
close down the conversation.

'And it helps,' he said finally.

'With what?'

'My frustration.' His mouth twisted. 'Not *that* kind.
I'm talking about my parents. I love them. They've always put me first and given me everything. But it just
frustrates me that I can't give them what they want.'

What do they want? The question formed on her
lips but she didn't need to ask it. She knew what they
wanted.

Her chest felt tight. Guiltily, she remembered the
conversation they'd had about telling their families
about her pregnancy. She'd been so wrapped up in her
own concerns she'd not even considered his wishes.

'Yes you can.' Reaching out, she took his hand. 'Tell
them about the baby. We can tell them now, if you like.'

His eyes met hers, then glanced away, and she pressed her hand protectively against her stomach.

Just for a moment, idiot that she was, she'd thought he was upset at having to keep their baby a secret from his parents, but actually he was worried about them learning the truth.

The shock of this discovery took her breath away.

'I suppose this isn't exactly what they planned,' she said flatly. He didn't reply, and she felt her pulse accelerate. 'Did they have someone else in mind?' She took a deep breath. 'Did you?'

'No—and no. But they had hopes.'

He smiled then, only it was a smile that made her feel hollow inside.

'They've always had hopes for me.'

'Then they must be very proud,' she said quickly, trying to ignore the needles of misery piercing her skin. 'You've built an empire.'

He nodded. 'They *are* proud. But they're very traditional...old-fashioned. To them, money and status is a bonus. It's family that matters.'

Kitty frowned. 'You're giving them a grandchild.'

He nodded, but there was nothing affirming in his body language. He looked taut and unconvinced.

'Is it because I'm English, not Cuban?'

He shook his head. 'My father will probably say that it's fate. That at least now there was a reason for banishing them to *La Yuma*.' Glancing at Kitty's baffled expression, he gave her a small, tight smile. 'The US.'

But it wasn't the slang that had confused her. Clearing her throat, she said, 'What do you mean, "banishing them"? Who banished them, and why?'

'The who is easy, it was me.' He stared down at her

hand entwined with his. 'The why is more complicated,' he said finally.

His voice was offhand, but she could feel the tension pulsing through his fingers into hers. She hesitated. She didn't know what the rules were for this kind of conversation in their kind of relationship. Or even if there were rules for their kind of relationship.

She lifted her chin, felt the pinpricks of panic starting to dissolve. *So you make the rules then,* she told herself.

'No, it's not.' she told him. 'You just start at the beginning and carry on till the end.'

The muscles of his arms trembled, and for half a second or so she thought he was going to pull away, but then he nodded slowly.

'I was twenty-three. I'd just finished my studies and my father wanted me to take over the business. He'd had a lot of health problems and he'd been pretty much holding on, waiting for me to step up. Only I didn't want to do it.' He grimaced. 'I was an only child, the son and heir, and I was spoilt and very much loved. I wanted to have fun and freedom, so I persuaded them to let me go to the US for a year.'

She squeezed his hand. 'What did you do?'

'Not much. I slept all day and partied all night.' He hesitated. 'That's where I met Celia. At a party. She was older than me. Cool. Hard to pin down. Nothing like anyone I'd ever met. I chased her for weeks before she agreed to go out with me.'

His jaw tightened.

'I thought everything would change once we were together, but it didn't. She moved into my apartment but quite often she'd just not come home. One time I got angry and she stormed off. I lost my head. I was so scared that I'd lost her that I ran out into the street in my boxer shorts but she'd gone. And then she wouldn't answer my calls or messages.'

He swallowed.

'The next day I got a call from my mum and I went home. They knew immediately that something was up, so I told them I was in love with Celia and that I was going to marry her.'

Kitty nodded as though she understood, but it hurt, hearing his pain. Hurt, too, knowing that he had been so in love. 'What happened?'

He looked down into her eyes. 'They were appalled. They tried to talk me out of it, told me I was too young. I got angry again and stormed off.' His face stiffened. 'But not before I'd taken my grandmother's engagement ring. I wanted to prove to Celia that I was serious—prove to my parents that I was an adult. When I got back to the US I found Celia and proposed to her, and she accepted. Then I rang my parents and told them I was getting married and staying in America.'

His face was like a mask.

'Two weeks later I came home early and found her in bed with the guy who lived down the hall. At first she cried, and then she got angry and told me it was my fault for being so needy and immature. That's when I asked her to give my grandmother's ring back. Only she said no, so I had to call my father. He sorted it out, but they were devastated and disappointed.'

'They were just worried about you,' she said gently.

He shook his head. 'I was stupid and naive. Too trusting and open. When I came back to Cuba I knew I had to change. And I did.'

She nodded and, reaching out, she touched the dark

fabric of his jacket. 'You wear your suits like armour.' She hesitated. 'So why did you "banish" your parents?'

He held her gaze. 'Being back in Cuba just got harder and harder. I couldn't be myself here.' Looking away, he breathed out slowly. 'You know how it is. We love life. Everyone talks and dances and flirts.'

He smiled stiffly, and she smiled back. 'I'd noticed.'

He shifted against her. 'Only I couldn't be like that anymore. It worked being autocratic and formal at work, but I couldn't be like that with my family and friends, so when my father got ill I used it as an excuse to move them to the US.'

His mouth twisted.

'They don't hate it, but they're really homesick. It would kill them, knowing I'm living here with you and that they aren't a part of it.' He shook his head. 'I've hurt them so much.'

'And that's why you wanted to marry me?' Kitty swallowed, tears forming behind her eyes. 'Not just to tie up loose ends?'

He nodded. 'It seemed like the perfect solution. I was never going to marry anyone for love, but I could be a husband to you, a father to our child, *and* give my parents what they want.'

Kitty swallowed past the lump in her throat. To be young and in love was beautiful, and she'd been so lucky with Jimmy. He'd been sweet and straightforward. But César had been betrayed and hurt so badly that he'd retreated behind a mask.

Only now the mask was gone.

But the scars hadn't. And she wasn't talking about the ones she could see.

'You're a good person,' she said softly. 'A good son.'

He looked pensive. 'I shouldn't have told you. I'm supposed to be supporting you, not the other way around.'

'I'm glad you did.' Reaching up, she stroked his face. 'We're here to support each other.' She took a breath. 'And that's what we're going to tell our families. That we're having a baby and we're taking our relationship one step at a time.'

He gazed down at her in silence, and then he pulled her against him and she felt the tension seep out of him.

'One step at a time,' he repeated. 'That sounds perfect.'

CHAPTER NINE

CLOSING HER LAPTOP, Kitty smiled slowly. Her heart was beating softly. Finally, after weeks of circling through her notes, she was finally making some progress. The characters of the two rums she'd been hired to create were taking form in her head, at least, and she had that same humming in her blood she'd had when she'd been making Blackstrap.

Of course she'd have to do some tastings back in Havana, and run it past César.

She glanced guiltily over her shoulder. True to his word, he had taken a step back from the business, so it seemed unfair of her to be working sneakily, but just like last time she was unstoppable.

Leaning over, she pushed the laptop underneath her lounger. She was lying on the veranda. Above her, an apricot sun was inching lazily across a completely cloudless blue sky. She felt drowsy with heat, and thirsty too, only moving felt like such an effort—and besides, she just wanted to lie there a little longer and keep thinking.

And thinking was really only possible when César wasn't around.

It felt as if he was always around now, even when

he wasn't. She thought back to the moment when she'd woken that morning. They'd woken early and made love, and then he had got up to go for a run and she had dozed, her body enveloped in the heat he'd left behind so that it had felt as though he was still pressing against her, his arm wrapping her tightly in the growing light.

Frowning, she shook her head. Up until yesterday her feelings for him had been neatly filed into categories. For her boss, she felt a mixture of admiration and awe. Alongside that, her body resonated with a fierce, sexual hunger for César her lover, but there was also a feeling of reassurance from the man who was the father of her baby. In some ways it had felt as if she was dealing with three different men.

But since opening up to her about his relationship with Celia and his guilt over his impulsive youthful behaviour he had changed, and now it was as though part of an invisible weight had been lifted. He seemed easier in himself, so that now she was seeing him as a whole person.

Only for some reason getting to know him better hadn't simplified her response, instead her feelings were now a swirl of confusion.

Her heart ached when she thought of how he must have felt when he'd found his fiancée in bed with another man. He had been young and alone in a foreign country, and he'd given his heart to a woman he'd thought felt the same way, only to learn that she'd betrayed him.

Remembering how he'd talked about hanging around on beaches with his mates, she felt a surge of anger. Now that she knew the full story, it was easy to imagine the younger César with his easy smile, messing around with his friends. No wonder he'd been driven to suppress that side of his character. He'd done it to protect himself from further pain, and to spare his family from being hurt and disappointed again. But in doing so he'd had to close himself off from the people he loved most.

Only not any more.

Her heart contracted. They had spoken to her family first. Of course her mum had cried a little, but her happiness had been obvious. She'd sensed that Bill was desperate to engage César with rum-related topics, so it hadn't been a long call, but she'd had a separate, private and more tearful conversation with Lizzie.

It had been so good to talk to her sister. Lizzie was so candid and certain about everything. 'You can't just marry *anyone*, Kitty,' she'd said firmly. I mean, why would you want to marry a jaw-droppingly handsome Cuban billionaire with a string of homes anyway?'

They had both burst out laughing.

'Seriously, though, there's only one reason to ever get married,' Lizzie had said, when finally they'd both calmed down enough to speak again. 'And when you feel it you know where to find a bridesmaid.'

Telling César's parents had actually been easier than she'd expected. They were delighted by news of their forthcoming grandchild, clearly devoted to their son, and prepared to embrace his unconventional relationship with Kitty.

And she'd seen how much their reaction had mattered to César. The tension which she had always taken to be a part of him, like the greenness of his eyes or the clean curve of his jaw, had eased a little. It felt as if together they'd begun to erase their pasts, and she was meeting him for the first time.

Her cheeks began to burn with a heat that had nothing to do with the sun. Except she wasn't about to erase the memory of their first meeting for anything.

'What are you thinking about?'

She glanced up, her heart suddenly beating too fast. César was leaning against the doorframe, his green eyes roaming slowly over her near-naked body. He'd obviously just got back from his run. His black T-shirt and shorts were damp with sweat, and his golden skin and the stripes of shadow and sunlight across his face made him look almost tigerish.

'Oh, nothing really,' she lied.

Unpeeling himself from the wood, he sauntered over and bent down to kiss her. His lips were soft, and instantly her blood seemed to turn to air. As he dropped down beside her on the lounger she took a small breath. Even though it was no longer new to her, his beauty still dazzled her.

'So why are you blushing?' he said softly.

She punched him lightly on the arm. 'I'm not blushing. I'm warm.'

His eyes met hers and then dropped to the veranda floor. 'Were you working?'

Her cheeks grew warm. 'I didn't mean to, but then I thought of something and it all started to come together.'

'I'm happy for you.' He held her gaze. 'I know how frustrating it is when something's just out of reach.'

She frowned. 'I'm not out of reach.'

There was a short silence, and then he smiled. 'No, you're not. And you weren't blushing because you'd been working.'

'I wasn't blushing,' she protested.

'It you don't tell me I'm going to have to read your mind.'

Cupping her face in his hand, he held her gaze, and, wriggling free, she started to laugh. 'Okay, fine—I was blushing. But I don't want to tell you what I was thinking about.'

'Why not?'

He started to nuzzle her neck, his fingers moving lightly over her skin, and she breathed out unsteadily. Now her whole body was growing warm. 'A woman should have some mystery.'

Raising his lips from her neck, he lifted his face. 'But I want to know everything about you,' he said softly.

Her pulse was beating out of time. There had been other moments before when he'd been gentle, like when she'd told him about Jimmy, so why did this feel different?

It wasn't. It shouldn't be.

The fact that he had opened up to her was obviously a positive, but he didn't love her, and she didn't love him, and that was what she wanted—what she needed. Because the flipside of love was a pain she couldn't go through again.

So it didn't matter that his words made her chest feel tight. Nothing had changed between them, and if that wasn't clear right now it was probably just down to what he'd told her yesterday playing on her mind. Even if he was saying things that went beyond the bedroom-based borders of their relationship—a relationship that would end when one of them tired of the other.

Or at least the physical side would end. Her hand slipped down to rest on her stomach. There would still always be this link between them.

Reaching up, she took hold of his T-shirt and pulled him closer. 'I was thinking about the first time we met.'

She watched his face still, as she'd known it would, but not before she caught something flickering across his eyes. It was there and gone before she had a chance to make sense of it, and it was easy to push it aside when his hand was warming her skin. To let herself be distracted by the fine dark hair on his wrists.

'Do you remember?'

'How could I forget?'

She felt his fingers slide over her stomach protectively.

'That evening is burned into my memory. Even when I shut my eyes I can still see you on that sofa.'

She shivered. Her body was starting to ache. 'I can see it too,' she whispered. 'But my eyes are open.'

They reached for one another at the same time.

Later, he re-tied the strings of her bikini and she smoothed his hair into some sort of order.

'It's the least I can do after ravishing you.' She smiled, wanting to tease him, liking the way one side of his mouth curved higher than the other when he smiled back at her.

'Thank you,' he said softly as she leaned back and admired her efforts. Lowering his mouth, he pressed a kiss to her hand. 'How do you feel about *barbacoas?* It's just that I got a call this morning from Pablo. He's a neighbour, and he and his wife Julia are some of my parents' oldest friends. They've invited us over to his estate for lunch.'

'Really?'

He lifted her hand, weaving his fingers through hers. 'I'm guessing my mother must have rung Julia and told her about us, but if you don't want to go it's not a problem.'

'Of course I want to go.' Glancing down at her bikini, she frowned. 'Will it be really formal? Because I don't have anything smart with me.'

He shook his head. 'No, not at all. It'll be fun—just food and dancing and dominos. Pretty much your average Cuban Saturday family gathering. They'll be loads of *niños* running around, the teenagers will all be eyeing one another up, and as soon as we walk through the door you and I will get cornered by the *abuelas.*'

He grimaced.

'You've heard of the Spanish Inquisition? Well, the Cuban *abuelas* have their own version. They'll be grilling me all afternoon and then serving *me* up with the *mojo* instead of the usual hog roast.'

She burst out laughing. 'I thought you said it was going to be fun?'

He grinned. 'I'm joking. I will probably have to answer a few questions—' his eyes gleamed '—but they'll spend most of the afternoon trying to feed you up.'

Two hours later Kitty was standing downstairs, waiting for César to join her. He'd had some clothes sent over for her when they'd decided to stay on the plantation, and she'd chosen a long apple-green dress covered in tiny leaves that Lizzie had bought her for her birthday last year. It was loose enough to wear in the heat, but it felt less casual than wearing a skirt and blouse.

In fact, maybe she could send Lizzie a photo of herself wearing it. She held her phone at arm's length, trying to fit herself into the frame and stay in focus, but it was harder than it looked.

'Do you want me to help?'

She turned. César was strolling towards her, a key fob dangling from his fingers. She stared at him blankly.

He frowned. 'I thought I'd drive—unless that's a problem?'

Her heart thumped inside her chest. She shook her head. It wasn't the thought of him driving that had caused her fingers to freeze around her phone. César was wearing pale green linen trousers and a cream shirt, rolled up to the elbows. He looked both cool and mouth-wateringly sexy.

'You're not wearing a suit,' she said unnecessarily.

He glanced down. 'No, I thought maybe I wouldn't today.'

She swallowed, her eyes snagging on the golden skin and corded muscles of his arms as he took a step towards her, his hand reaching for hers, his green gaze moving slowly from her eyes down to her toes.

'You look beautiful.'

He pulled her towards him, twirling her expertly into the warm solidity of his body, curving his arm around her waist so that the soft green of his trousers seemed to melt into the leaves of her dress.

'We match,' he said softly.

His green eyes were intent on her face and she realised that they were both smiling. She felt that sudden tightening in her chest, except that it wasn't exactly a feeling of tightness but more as though a balloon of happiness was swelling beneath her ribs, so that she could almost feel herself lifting up off the ground.

And why *shouldn't* she feel happy? For such a long time it had felt as if she was just going through the motions. It hadn't even been grief—just a sense that life was passing her by while she was treading water and trying to stay afloat.

But now she had a job she loved in a country that was starting to feel like a second home. She was having a baby, and in César she had a beautiful, tireless lover. That was enough.

It was a short drive to the Montañez estate. As they walked into the garden, he turned and caught her eye and she nearly burst out laughing, because it was exactly how he'd described it—right down to the teenagers eyeballing one another and the hog roast cooking slowly in the afternoon sun.

As predicted, César did get cornered and cross-examined, but even though she couldn't follow every word of the conversation it was clear that he was doted on by the *abuelas*.

Lunch was served in the shade of the house. The centrepiece of the meal was the pork, accompanied by *chicharrones*—bite-size pieces of crackling which tasted incredible with the citrusy *mojo* sauce—but there were also huge platters of avocado and pineapple salad, and of course *congri*, the famous rice and beans dish that was both delicious and comforting.

Leaning back against the extra cushion that her hostess, Julia, had insisted that she have, Kitty gazed down the table, her eyes drawn to where César had been dragged by the other men to smoke cigars.

It was the first time he had left her side all afternoon. When they'd arrived he'd led her between the clumps of guests, introducing her in both Spanish and English, acting as a translator when necessary, and all the time his arm had rested lightly against her back.

She knew, of course, that he was just being polite—

attentive in the same way as when he'd gone and found her a non-alcoholic drink—but even so she had felt herself responding, wanting to draw closer, to lean into him.

Right now he was lounging in his chair, talking, his green eyes dark beneath the shaded canopy, surrounded by men smoking, and sipping *ron*. She watched as he said something and a burst of laughter floated towards her, momentarily drowning out the more sedate sound of the dominos clicking against the tabletop.

He held up his hand, tilting the rum so that the men watching him all tipped their heads to one side, and she found herself smiling. With his gaze fixed on the glass in his hand, and his arm resting casually against the back of the chair, he looked less like a CEO and more like his Roman namesake: Caesar addressing his senators.

Behind them on the lawn some of the children were playing chase, but two of them—a girl and a younger boy, brother and sister maybe—stood side by side eating *coquitos*, their eyes wide as the others zig-zagged past them.

Kitty watched as the boy held up his caramel-covered hand, frowning.

The girl shook her head. *'Puaj! No me toques!'* Turning she tugged the jacket of the man nearest to César—Pablo's nephew, Jorge. *'Papi, Javi está todo pegajoso!'*

Picking up a napkin, the man reached down—but his son was too quick and, laughing, grabbed César's leg and hauled himself onto his lap, burying his face against his shirt.

Oh, no. Kitty held her breath. She could see the sticky smears even from where she was sitting. But, waving away Jorge's apologies, César grinned, and then, gently grabbing the little boy's hands, he held them out to be wiped clean.

Her chest was aching. He was so sweet. His patience, his gentleness, reminded her of Jimmy—and yet for the first time ever she couldn't picture Jimmy in her head. His familiar features seemed to have faded, no longer sharp but blurred and growing fainter.

Around her, the noise of the party faded too, drowned out by the hammering of her heart. She stared at César, mesmerised. This was what he would be like with his own child. The thought made her whole body swell with happiness, so that she couldn't hold in her smile. Only there was a lump in her throat too. For, even though she knew there was no point in thinking it, it was impossible not to imagine that if they were a real couple then together they would be a family—the kind of family that she'd dreamed about for so long.

As though feeling her gaze, César glanced up, his eyes seeking hers. It was the kind of private look that only couples shared—a mix of tenderness and understanding that made her feel dizzy. Except they weren't a real couple. Just two people taking one step at a time...

She managed to keep smiling as César stood up and strolled over to where she sat, concern in his eyes. 'Is everything okay? You look a little pale.'

She nodded, still smiling. 'I'm always pale.'

He sat beside her, his green gaze resting on her face, and then, reaching out, he rested his hand lightly on her stomach. 'If it's a girl I want her to have your hair.'

Ignoring the way her pulse skipped forward, she cleared her throat. 'And if it's a boy I'll let you clean him up when he's been eating *coquitos*.'

Grinning, he leaned forward and plucked a beautiful

white flower from the arrangement on the table. 'Here.' Gently he slotted it into her hair. 'My *mariposa*.'

She felt her heart bump against her ribs. 'I can't be your *mariposa*. It's the Cuban national flower and I'm a foreigner.'

His eyes collided with hers. 'Actually, it's a foreigner too. It comes from India. In the Revolution, Cuban women who helped the rebels used to wear them in their hair.'

'Well, I'm helping you with your rums, so does that make you a rebel?' she asked teasingly.

'Not today.' He grimaced. 'Today I need Julia to report back to my mum that I was the perfect gentleman. Speaking of which—would you like to dance?' He glanced down at his shirt. 'Or am I too sticky?'

She swallowed past the lump in her throat. 'You're not sticky, you're sweet,' she said.

And, standing up, she let him lead her beneath the huge shaded gazebo to where couples were circling to salsa music. Curving his hand around her waist, he pulled her close.

'Everyone's looking at us,' she whispered.

'Not us.' He gazed down at her, his green eyes dark and intent. 'They know me far too well to find me in any way interesting. It's you they're looking at.'

She felt her pulse slow. If only she could freeze time, capture this moment. Heart pounding, she stared at him, wanting desperately to memorise every detail of his face.

'Yes, because I'm with you,' she said lightly. 'Mr Big Shot from Havana.'

Havana—the word reverberated in the air between them. Since deciding to stay at the plantation neither of them had really talked about when they were going to go back. She knew he must be in contact with his office but, true to his word, he'd taken the promised step back from work and it hadn't seemed to come up in conversation.

Only of course they couldn't stay here for ever…

Judging by César's expression, he was clearly thinking the same thing. His next remark confirmed her suspicion.

'Talking of which, I suppose we should think about heading back fairly soon.'

He was staring right into her eyes and she tried to smile, to take his casual remark at face value even though she felt as though her heart had relocated to her throat.

'Yes, I suppose we should,' she agreed.

There was a short silence, as though he was waiting for her to say something more, or maybe to say something else himself, but then finally he nodded.

'Do you want to go today?' She braced herself for his reply.

He frowned. 'No, there's no rush. We can drive back tomorrow.' He paused, his face stilling, and she sensed that he was working through something in his head. 'Actually, I don't think we'll take the car. I don't know if I told you, but I have a yacht—'

She raised an eyebrow. 'Of course you do.'

He grinned. 'It might be fun to sail her down to Havana.'

'Is this a good time for me to tell you that I'm really bad at tying knots?'

'You are?' His eyes gleamed. 'That's a coincidence— so am I. Maybe we should spend tonight in the cabin, practising a few,' he said softly.

* * *

Raising his hand to block out the glare of the sun, César gazed at the turquoise sea. It looked perfect.

He felt a thrill of anticipation—could almost taste the adrenaline. It had been months since he'd had a chance to get out on the water, and it felt great to feel the spray on his face. He felt lighter, as though the chains of his youthful stupidity were no longer restraining him. And they weren't—thanks to Kitty. She had freed him, forced him to let go of the pain and the guilt, and now he felt at peace with his past.

And yet something still felt off-key and unfinished.

He looked across the deck to the waves beyond. Usually being on the yacht transcended his mood, but of course usually he sailed alone. His jaw tightened. Maybe inviting her on to the boat had been a bad idea.

For him, sailing was both a release and a challenge. He loved pitting himself against the strength of the sea and the pull of the wind, and he liked that version of himself.

He pictured Kitty's naked body in the cabin below. Then again...

'You look like a pirate.'

He turned. Kitty was standing behind him, wearing nothing but a bikini and one of his shirts. A couple of weeks of careful exposure to the sun had turned her skin the palest gold, and her breasts had rounded out a little. He felt his body stir.

Grabbing hold of the shirt, he tugged her towards him, a pulse of heat tiptoeing across his skin. 'And you look like some incredibly sexy Girl Friday.'

She screwed up her mouth. 'If that's some misguided attempt to get me to scrub the decks, you can forget it. My talents lie elsewhere.'

He grinned. 'Yes, they do.'

'I was talking about making rum.'

'So was I,' he lied. Lifting his hand, he stroked her face. 'Did you get some sleep?'

She nodded. 'I went out like a light. I think it must be the—' Her forehead creased.

He frowned. 'What is it?'

'I just thought of a name for one of the rums.'

Watching her pupils flare, he felt his blood grow lighter. She was genuinely excited.

'Diabolito—you know...?'

'The pirate.' He nodded slowly. 'I like it.'

'You do?'

'Yes, I do—and, what's more, I've just thought of a name for the other one.' His stomach flipped with a rush of anticipation more intense than any skydive. 'What do you think of Mariposa?'

Her smoky eyes widened and a flush of colour spread over her cheeks. 'I think it's beautiful,' she said shakily.

For a moment they stared at one another, and then she glanced over his shoulder and frowned again.

'Have we stopped?'

He grinned. 'Spoken like a true sailor. It's called dropping anchor— and, yes, we have. I thought maybe we could do a little snorkelling.'

The look of surprise on her face made his grin widen.

'Boring fact—Cuba has the second largest reef in the world after the Great Barrier Reef.'

And exploring it with Kitty would be fun. The fact that it would delay their return to Havana was of course just coincidental.

He could see the longing in her eyes, but she started to shake her head. 'I don't actually know how to.'

'It's easy.' He took her hand. 'I promise. All you have to do is breathe. You'll be great.'

'Will I?'

Her grey eyes looked almost silver in the sunlight, and her expression was so open and trusting that it hurt him to look at her.

'Of course—and I'll be right there beside you.' He pointed across the deck. 'All you need is a mask and a snorkel and some flippers. Try the orange ones—they're a little smaller.'

His heart was thumping against his ribs. The idea had come to him while she was sleeping and now, watching her pick up a pair of flippers, he felt stupidly excited. He didn't know why, but he wanted to be the one to introduce Kitty to the undersea world.

No, that wasn't true. He *did* know why. She'd had such a terrible time. She'd known heartbreak and loss and he wanted to see her happy. He wanted to *make* her happy. And this would be something special just between them.

Turning, he walked over to where Kitty was standing. She had her back to him, her head tilted to one side, and the hem of his shirt was riding high on her thighs as she gazed abstractedly at a face mask.

He stood for a moment and admired the flaring curve of her bottom, and then his gaze stilled as she rotated her hand and he watched her small, delicate fingers cup and caress the mask. Her touch was light, almost reverent, and he felt his felt his body stir, the blood starting to pound hot and fast as he remembered how she had touched him in the same way but for another, more intimate reason just a few hours ago.

'Ready?' he called.

She turned and, smiling shyly, she nodded.

As they swam side by side he felt both incredibly protective and captivated by Kitty's wide-eyed excitement. It had been such a long time since he'd allowed himself to be so open, but with her it was easy—not just to reveal his own pleasure but to enjoy hers. And there was a rainbow of reef life to enjoy in the warm, clear waters: yellow and blue angelfish, coral-coloured parrotfish and zebra-striped spadefish. It was as though the sea had decided to put on a cabaret.

And Kitty looked enchanted.

'I never thought it would be like that,' she said as they enjoyed lunch on deck. 'I thought it would be dark and gloomy and that all the fish would be scared of us. But they're not.'

He smiled. He couldn't imagine anything being scared of Kitty. 'It's because they're still not that used to divers. Probably because it's on our doorstep, Cubans themselves don't bother with diving that much.'

'What's it like if you go deeper?'

He grinned. 'Cold! That's why you wear a wetsuit. But it's amazing—like a whole new world you didn't even know existed.'

She shivered. 'I'm not sure I'm ready for that.'

Watching her face, he felt his throat tighten. He felt like a tuning fork. Everything she was feeling seemed to resonate through him too, so that her happiness was his happiness, her pain became his pain. It was a strange, unsettling sensation, and even though he couldn't give a name to it he knew it was dangerous.

His heart began to beat faster. There were safer ways of seeking danger.

He glanced past her at the still sea. 'Actually, there's a wreck just along the coast from here, and as we're in the area I thought I might go take a look.'

'On your own?'

He heard and ignored the confusion in her voice. He'd solo-dived before. It was a more risky than diving in a group, but right now that was what he needed. He shrugged. 'Even if you weren't pregnant, it wouldn't be safe for a first deep dive.' He hesitated. 'I don't have to go…'

'No, it's fine. I want you to go.' She gave him a quick, tight smile. 'Really.'

They anchored twenty minutes later.

The coastline was more rugged here, and the water was choppier, and he could see from Kitty's expression that she was having second thoughts.

'I'll be fine.' Taking her hands, he pulled her against him and kissed her lightly on the lips. 'I know what I'm doing. I've done a lot of dives and this is pretty shallow.'

'How long will you be?'

'Forty minutes?' He glanced at her face, then at his watch. 'I'll be back up in half an hour.'

He was desperate to go. Desperate to prove that *this* was what his life had been lacking. This rush of exhilaration—part fear, part anticipation. Kitty might be captivating in so many ways, but this was what made his pulse race.

Holding his mask and regulator in place with his palm, he stepped off the side of the yacht into the water.

Watching him disappear beneath the waves, Kitty felt her chest tighten. It was stupid to feel so tense. He knew what he was doing.

She took a breath. It was only half an hour. Thirty short minutes. Shorter than the time it took her to wash and dry her hair.

She glanced down at her phone, at the timer she'd set as he jumped into the water. Twenty-five minutes now.

There was no point in worrying. There wasn't anything she could do if something went wrong down there. But it made her feel dizzy just thinking about all the things that could go wrong.

Life wasn't kind or fair—she knew that—and the ocean was a cruel place. But César was an experienced diver, and the sea had been kind to her.

Thinking back to how a group of beautiful angelfish had swum right up to her mask, she smiled. They had been so gentle, so curious, and the warm water had felt incredibly relaxing and safe. Her stomach gave a little flip. That was what it must be like for their baby.

Resting her hand against the slight curve of her belly, she glanced down at the timer and breathed out slowly. Only ten minutes to go now.

Which was just enough time for her to take a few pictures to send to Lizzie.

She was reading her sister's response to the photos when the timer went off.

Feeling a rush of relief, she made her way to the swim platform. She stood gazing down at the water, her heartbeat filling her head. *Where was he?*

She glanced down at her phone. He was five minutes later than he'd said he would be.

Her heartbeat sped up. An ache was spreading out from her heart—an ache she remembered, an ache she had never wanted to feel again. She glanced back at the phone. Now he was eight minutes late.

Did he have enough oxygen?

A hot and slippery panic was crawling over her skin. She felt sick and scared.

What if something had happened to him?

The thought was unbearable.

It hurt like an actual physical pain, as though a crack was opening up inside her. But why did it hurt so badly? It was completely disproportionate, excessive, unreasonable, and it didn't make any sense. They barely knew one other and they weren't even a 'real' couple.

She thought back to the lunch party, and to the way her eyes had met his along the length of the table.

No, it didn't make any sense, unless—

Unless she loved him.

She breathed out unsteadily. Her heart felt as though it was about to burst out of her chest and her whole body was vibrating with shock and acceptance and joy at her silent admission.

But of *course* she loved him.

Every thought, every action, every feeling she had led back to him. Even when he wasn't there she could conjure him up, fully formed, inside her head.

Only how had it happened? She had never expected to feel this way again. She'd thought that life had given and then taken away everything it had to give. But then this man had stepped into her path—or rather she had stepped into his—and now she could feel love and hope working through her veins as she gazed down at the sea.

And then, just like that, he was there, bursting through the surface of the water, his dark hair sleek against his head. As he pulled himself up onto the platform the blood seemed to drain from her body with relief.

His eyes, so green, so familiar, so necessary, locked with hers. 'What is it? Did something happen?'

She hesitated. Really though, what could she say? *Yes, I just realised I love you.*

She wasn't feeling that brave right now.

'You're late.'

'I know.'

He pulled her against him, and the chill of his usually warm body was a shock.

'I was under the boat and I noticed a couple of dents in the hull.' His hand tightened in her hair. 'I just wanted to check them out.'

His voice was tense, distant, as though he was still beneath the water.

She nodded. She felt exhausted. But he was alive, and he was here, and that was all that mattered.

They reached Havana by mid-evening.

As they followed the inevitable traffic diversion through the centre César had to grip the edge of his seat to stop himself knocking on the glass behind Rodolfo's head and asking him to take them back to the boat.

After the peace and isolation of the plantation the city felt incredibly loud and bright, and maybe Kitty felt the same, he thought as they headed back to the estate. She had been quiet in the car. In fact, she'd been quiet since the dive.

Later, she was quiet during dinner too. But maybe it wasn't just bodies that needed to decompress after a dive. Perhaps emotionally it was hard to adjust to ordinary life when moments earlier you'd been in a thrilling underwater world.

'If you like we could take the boat out next weekend.

There's a nature reserve just up the coast with turtles and stingrays. Sometimes even manatees.'

She stared up at him, her thoughts clearly elsewhere. 'That would be lovely.' She hesitated. 'I'm sorry that you didn't get longer in the water.'

'It's fine.'

His heart clenched as he thought back to the dive, to the moment when he'd realised that something was wrong. Tension had been building in his chest, his blood pulsing inside his head, and at first he'd thought it was his mouthpiece. But of course it hadn't been.

She bit her lip. 'You didn't say much about it.'

He frowned, then rubbed a hand over his face. 'It was different from usual.'

'In what way?'

His heart was thumping now. The tension was back. Earlier, in the water, he'd forced himself to go deeper, to do what he always did, what he'd always done—flee the feeling. Only this time he hadn't run, he'd swum.

But the feeling had stayed with him. And there, in the shifting currents of the Atlantic, he'd realised that it didn't matter how far he swam. For years now he'd kept pushing his body to the limit—diving, climbing, base-jumping—always seeking the next thrill, constantly needing to go deeper, faster, higher. Only for the first time he had asked himself why?

Could it be that all those physical challenges were just an attempt to fill a void? The void left by his decision not to pursue the normal goals of adult life—marriage, falling in love, having a family?

If so, then they were no longer necessary.

He'd reached the wreck and then, using the currents,

made his way over and around it, trying to escape the pressure in his chest, choosing not to give it a name.

Now, though, with her beautiful, serious grey eyes on his face, he didn't want to escape, and he was tired of fleeing.

Reaching out, he took her hand. 'Look, Kitty. I don't know how to say this—'

She stared at him, her fingers stiffening.

'So I'm just going to start at the beginning and carry on to the end.'

'Okay,' she whispered.

'I wanted you from the first moment I saw you, and I tried to stay away only I couldn't. So I came back. And then you told me you were pregnant, and I wanted to be there for the baby, so I asked you to marry me. But I didn't love you.'

'I know.' Her eyes were wide and bright. 'I know how you feel, César.'

His grip tightened around her hand. 'Only today, when I went down to the wreck, I kept expecting to feel how I usually do. A little bit nervous, maybe, and excited. But I didn't.'

His mouth twisted.

'The whole dive just didn't feel right. I kept thinking something was missing. And then I realised...' He paused. 'I realised that it was you. I missed you, and what I was feeling was loneliness. I told myself I was being stupid, that it was the dive talking. Only when I got out of the water I felt better. I felt whole again.'

She cleared her throat. 'What are you saying?'

'I'm saying that I still want to marry you.' He let out a shaky breath. 'But this time it's because I love you.'

'You *love* me?' For a moment she stared at him blankly, and then slowly she withdrew her hand from his.

Striving for calm, he opened his mouth—but his words stayed unspoken as she started to shake her head.

'But I never asked for your love and I don't need it. I don't want it.'

'Kitty—'

He reached across the table, but she jerked backwards.

Still shaking her head, she got to her feet, scraping her chair across the floor. 'I'm sorry, César, but I don't love you.'

The chair fell backwards, and as it hit the floor he watched, heart hammering, body frozen, as she turned and ran from the room.

CHAPTER TEN

KITTY MOVED BLINDLY through the house, the lie echoing inside her head. Her heart was racing, her blood pounding incessantly.

He loved her and she loved him.

So why had she turned and run from him?

But that question didn't need answering.

She thought back to when she'd been waiting for him on the boat.

Waiting.

Worrying.

Hurting.

She stopped at the bottom of the staircase, blinking furiously.

Earlier, when she'd realised that she loved César, it had been a shock. For years she had lived believing that she would never love again. She'd shut down that part of her life. And then she'd moved here to Cuba, and suddenly there had been César, and now she was pregnant, and her world had started to grow warm again, and the ice around her heart had begun to melt.

It had felt exciting, picturing the two of them together, but now she could see that she had just tricked herself into thinking she had moved on and was ready for love.

She wasn't.

All she'd been doing was painting a picture in her head of a fantasy of love in a faraway place with a tall, dark, handsome stranger who made her heart beat faster.

César telling her that he loved her had made it real.

Too real.

She couldn't breathe.

Fantasy love didn't hurt, but real love did—because real love had to exist in the real world, where life was cruel and random. And that was why she had to leave now.

Her feet were moving of their own accord, up the stairs and into her bedroom. If she stayed, she wouldn't be able to resist him; she didn't want to resist him. But she couldn't love a man who lived the way he did. He was a risk-taker, and loving him would mean accepting she could lose him, and that was a risk she couldn't take—a pain she didn't ever want to feel again.

Only it hurt so much to think that she was going to have to leave.

Trying to hold back the tears that were threatening to spill over, she found her suitcase and began grabbing handfuls of her clothes. It was the only way.

'What are you doing?'

César's voice broke into the tumult of her thoughts. Her heart froze. She hadn't expected César to follow her. Why would he when she'd so inexplicably thrown his love back in his face?

Watching the light in his beautiful green eyes dim, she had wanted to take his hand and retract her words, to go to him and pull him close. But she had no right to do any of those things—not now, not ever—and the pain of knowing that, and of knowing that one day another woman would cradle his head in her lap, comfort him at the end of a long day, was her penance. It was necessary and right.

Only now he was here.

'I'm packing. I need to go home.'

'To England?'

The bruise in his voice wrenched at something inside her and, gripping the handle of her suitcase, she felt a tear slide down her cheek.

She swiped it away.

Please let him leave. Please don't make me have to look at him.

'Yes, to England. And nothing you say is going to change my mind.'

'Can't we talk about this?'

'There's no point. There's nothing to say.'

'I can't let you go, Kitty. Not like this. It's late, and you're upset.'

She shook her head and she heard him breathe out unsteadily.

'Then I'll go. I'll get a hotel.'

'No.' She turned. 'Why should you leave? It's your home.'

'It's your home too.'

She tried not to look at him, but she just couldn't stop herself. 'It's not. It never was. It just felt like it could be when we were at the plantation—'

He took a step forward. His green eyes were fixed on her face, and he looked pale and shaken. 'Nothing's changed except our location.'

'No, *everything's* changed.' She felt a flash of panic. She could feel herself wavering, wanting to believe what he was saying, longing to trust the hope in his eyes.

'Because I told you I love you?'

'And I told *you* that I don't believe in love,' she said.

He reached for her hand. 'No, you said you can't believe in love, that you can't feel that way again.'

He was right. She could remember saying the words—saying them when she had been still in shock from finding out that she was pregnant with his baby.

'But you do love me, Kitty. I know you do. And I know we can make this work.'

She tried to pull her hand away, but he didn't let go.

'So why are you running away?'

She didn't reply, and his eyes searched her face.

'Is it guilt? Do you think you don't deserve to be happy again? Because you do. You deserve it more than anyone I've ever known. You've been through so much, and you've been so strong and brave.'

Brave.

The word tasted bitter in her mouth.

Breathing out unsteadily, she looked up at him and shook her head. 'I'm not brave. I'm the opposite of brave. You want to know why I can't marry you? It's because I'm scared.'

He stared at her in silence, his eyes digging into hers. 'Kitty, I don't—'

Tugging her hand free, she took a step backwards. 'I know. You don't understand. And I get that. I get that you need things that I can't give you.' Her eyes caught sight of the thin raised scar on his arm. 'You live your life taking risks. You don't feel fear. I knew that the first time we met.'

Gazing down at Kitty's pale, strained face, César felt his skin tighten. Was that what she believed? He wanted to laugh, except there was something blocking his throat.

He thought back to the years he'd spent masking his easy-going trusting nature—the years he'd spent avoiding romantic attachments. Of course the sexual need had been there, and he'd taken care of that. Only he wasn't just talking about the women who had briefly shared his bed but never his life. Riding bikes, jumping out of planes, diving to the sea bed—they had all been a way to test his limits, to make his heart beat faster.

In a way that didn't actually threaten his heart in the emotional sense.

And somehow, over the years, he'd come to believe that it was enough—that the high of reaching the peak of a mountain was the same as the rush of seeing the face of the woman you loved light up when she saw you walk in the room.

Only it wasn't. And deep down he'd always known that. But he hadn't been able to admit it to himself. Hadn't been able to admit that that he chose to take risks with his life because he was scared of risking his heart. Scared of reaching out. Scared of sharing his life. Scared of trying for happily-ever-after and for ever.

He looked at Kitty.

But he was tired of being scared. And he was going to fight for Kitty even if that meant laying his feelings bare.

'You're wrong,' he said quietly.

'I know all about fear. And not the kind of fear you're talking about.'

His chest tightened. 'Do you remember when we were at the plantation and my father called and we argued about me climbing El Capitan? You asked me why I wanted to do something like that.'

She nodded. 'You said it helped you forget about work and about how you felt you'd let your parents down.'

'That's what I told you.' He cleared his throat. 'And I suppose on some level I was telling you the truth. But it's not the whole truth.' His pulse accelerated. 'After Celia I was scared of being myself. I was scared to trust my own judgement. I was scared of falling in love. And I hated feeling like that. I hated letting fear govern my behaviour. I hated being a coward.'

Reaching out, he took her hand again.

'And that's why I climb rock faces without a rope, why I pushed myself to the limit. It was so I could prove *to myself* that I wasn't a coward. But the truth is I was still a coward. I was still living in the past, hiding behind the bikes and the boats, still scared...'

The concern in her eyes made his heart swell.

'And maybe if you hadn't been out on that road that evening I'd still be scared.' His fingers tightened around hers. 'Before I met you I was living a lie, pretending to everyone that my life was exactly how I wanted it to be. But I wasn't really living. I was just carving up each week into days, and each day into hours, and filling them up so I didn't have to face my fears. And then I met you and everything I thought I wanted was worthless. Meaningless.'

He breathed out unsteadily and, lifting her hand, he pressed it gently against his lips.

'You know earlier today, when I was diving, I realised that nothing makes my heart beat as fast as you do. And all of that, and all of this—my business, my wealth—I could give it all up in a heartbeat. Because it doesn't mean anything unless we're together. You and me and the baby.'

Kitty could hardly breathe.

You and me and the baby.

She stared at him, tears burning her eyes. César wasn't the only one living in the past. And like him she'd been viewing that past selectively as though through the wrong end of a telescope. Her vision had shrunk and her memories had focused on the sadness of losing Jimmy, not on the happiness of loving him, so that she'd become terrified of loving again. Only she'd never stopped loving that whole time. She loved her family, and she loved this baby growing inside her, and she loved César too.

And he was right. It would be the same in England as in Havana. Changing the location wouldn't change how she felt. Nothing could change that.

Her heart was beating out of time, aching with a love she could finally express. 'That's all I want too.'

Her tears were falling now, but she let them fall, and as he pulled her against him her tears mingled with his.

'I love you.' He kissed her fiercely. 'I love you so much.'

'And I love you too.'

For a moment they just gazed at one another, breathing in each other's happiness, and then, reaching down, Kitty twisted his wrist to look at his watch.

'It's the same time in Florida as it is here, so I guess your parents will be asleep, won't they?'

César shook his head. 'Probably not. They still eat late, and they always have a siesta—'

'And what time is it in England?'

He frowned. 'It's about five o'clock in the morning.'

'Then we should probably call your parents first.'

'We should?'

She bit her lip. Her heart was pounding. 'Well, you want to invite them to the wedding, don't you?'

He stared at her blankly. 'The wedding…?'

'Unless you want to wait until after the baby's born?' she said softly.

His eyes, those beautiful green eyes she loved so much, rested on her face.

'Are you asking me to marry you?'

She nodded slowly. 'I wasn't sure you'd ask me a third time.'

Reaching into his trouser pocket, he pulled out a small round box and opened it. 'I was never going to stop asking you.'

She felt her heart backflip. 'Oh, César, it's beautiful.'

She watched, mesmerised, as he slid the sapphire and diamond ring shakily onto her finger, and then putting his hand under her chin, he lowered his mouth to hers and kissed her gently. Breaking away, he stared down at her, his green eyes transparent with love and hope.

'That was a yes, by the way.'

Her eyes met his and she nodded slowly.

'Yes, it was. It is,' she said. 'It definitely is.'

And, stroking his face, she kissed him back.

* * * * *

COMING SOON!

We really hope you enjoyed reading this book. If you're looking for more romance, be sure to head to the shops when new books are available on

Thursday 3rd October

To see which titles are coming soon, please visit

millsandboon.co.uk/nextmonth

MILLS & BOON

Coming next month

THE SICLIAN'S SURPRISE LOVE-CHILD
Carol Marinelli

Back in Rome, Nico wasn't certain he had read things right and was immediately on the phone.

Aurora had resigned.

Aurora Eloise Messina. Now aged twenty-five. With a passion for the hotel like no other and a hunger to succeed, had left.

It made no sense.

He knew full well that she was furious with him. And after the stunt she had pulled Nico had been furious too and had stayed well back.

But his anger was fading now—so much so that whenever he re-read that note he almost smiled.

'Why did she resign?' he asked.

'She was headhunted.'

Vincenzo sounded taken aback that the rather absent owner of the business was immediately on the phone to him the moment the email went out.

'By whom?'

'Aurora would not say. Apparently she was tired of her ideas being dismissed.'

They had *not* been dismissed. Had she turned up for dinner that night then she would have known that.

Nico called her. 'What's all this?'

'Scusi?' Aurora asked.

She was sitting in her little pink bedroom as she awaited a taxi to take her to the station.

Her parents had not taken the news of their daughter's pregnancy well at all—especially as Aurora refused to name the father. A terrible row had ensued.

Nico had been right: her parents *did* snoop, and they had gone through her phone and found the dating app she had downloaded in Rome.

And now she had Nico on the phone.

It was too much for her nerves today.

'Why have you resigned without speaking first with me?' he demanded.

'Nico, I resigned and I have left. I don't have to answer to you when you are no longer my boss.'

'All right, then. Forget that I was once your boss and tell *me*. Why did you resign?'

'So from what standpoint are we talking, Nico? As friends?' Aurora's voice was incredulous and angry, though she struggled to keep the hurt from it. 'Because we are *not* friends, Nico. You yourself told me we could never be.'

'Aurora—'

'Or are we speaking as lovers?' she interrupted. 'But that can't be because you have so many—surely you don't expect them all to give you career updates?'

'Aurora!'

She would not let him in. 'Or are we in a *relationship*, Nico? Oh, but that's right—no. Because you don't want one. You told me—'

'And *you* told me you would never leave Silibri.'

'I was sixteen years old when I said that. Tell me, Nico, is that the only reason you decided not to marry me?'

Silence.

As always, his silence killed her.

She wanted to curl up on her bed and weep into the phone.

Tell him. Tell him about the baby. Tell him that you have never felt so lonely nor so scared.

No!

And Aurora knew why she did not.

'I have to go, Nico. The taxi will come soon.'

It wasn't a lie.

She went downstairs. Her case stood at the front door and her parents sat at the table, looking at the photos the estate agent had taken of her *nonna*'s home.

The home meant for her and Nico.

Continue reading
THE SICILIAN'S SURPRISE LOVE-CHILD
Carol Marinelli

Available next month
www.millsandboon.co.uk

LET'S TALK
Romance

For exclusive extracts, competitions
and special offers, find us online:

 facebook.com/millsandboon

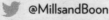 @MillsandBoon

@MillsandBoonUK

Get in touch on 01413 063232